The Price of a Promise

The Bad Boys of Wall Street: a Prequel

Ember Leigh

About 'The Price of a Promise'

Their love never stood a chance...

Axel Fairchild is the eternal outsider, both in his elite MBA program and in the world of NYC finance. Powering through on charm, swagger, and smarts has always worked for him—and it's poised to pay off in a big way as he prepares to launch his very own finance business with his brothers after graduation. There's only one thing left on his to-do list: prying the love of his life, Cora Margulis, away from her controlling and manipulative family.

Cora loves Axel's brash confidence and the way he turns her privileged world upside down. He's a breath of fresh air in the stuffy, elite enclave she's lived in her entire life. As she approaches the end of her MBA program and her father pressures her to join the ranks of their realty empire, Cora can see her escape hatch. The future beyond the luxurious world she's always known scares her, but with Axel at her side, she knows they can create the future of their dreams—together.

But the Margulis family is famous for bending people to their will behind closed doors. The closer Axel and Cora inch to graduation, the more oppressive the pressure grows from Cora's family to choose the right path. The only thing standing in the way of Cora and Axel's happily-ever-after is Allan Margulis. And he won't stop until he gets Cora in his back pocket and Axel is a ruined wreck.

CONTENTS

AUTHOR'S NOTE

**Billionaires. Bad boys. Bleeding hearts.
These outsiders are known as the Bad Boys of Wall Street.**

The Price of a Promise is the prequel novella to the Bad Boys of
Wall Street series. This series is best read in order, since the drama
is chronological and cumulative throughout the books. Start this
steamy forbidden romance between the wealthy NYC heroine and
the Kentucky boy from the wrong side of the tracks. Their love story
begins in the Price of the Promise and concludes eight years later in
The Price of Revenge.

CONTENT WARNING

-mentions of suicide

CHAPTER ONE

AXEL

"Wait, Axel. I'm almost there."

"Yeah? By the goth guys playing accordion or up by the vegan punks?"

Cora laughed in that way that sounded like angels sighing. Through the phone, I could hear the churn of the ocean on the West Coast. "The vegan punks."

"Shit, girl. You are almost there."

Cora's wispy breaths through the phone grew more labored. I pinched my eyes shut so I could imagine her—traipsing through the sand on Venice Beach, squinting against the too-bright sunshine of a November California day, which she claimed was against nature for the born-and-bred New York native that she was. She lived in Stanford, but liked to make the trek to LA on occasion for the shopping and the beaches.

"Hurry it up, sweet cheeks," I chided, grinning to myself as I sat on Coopers Beach in the Hamptons. This was our thing. The way we stayed connected, despite the staggering distance. Twenty-five hundred physical miles meant nothing if we were both standing on beaches facing the ocean. It was the voodoo that kept us together while we weathered grad school on opposite coasts.

Weekly beach visits and the occasional cross-country visit. But only when we could find the right alibi.

"Okay. I'm here." She sighed exaggeratedly and this time, I imagined her slumping down into the sand. In my mind's eye, I was there with her. Ready to catch her, to wrap my arms around her and find that perfect nook where she existed in my arms. The one that let me bury my face in the side of her lush, dark-chocolate locks and get drunk on her sweet clementine scent. Holding her like that was the only way to calm my racing heart when my anxiety stalked like a predator. When she was in my arms, I felt like I could fully grasp the roots of my future; like I could look up and watch the blossoms of my happiness unfold.

One of the many ways I knew Cora wasn't just a good fit for me but the one and only.

I planned to tell her soon. The moment the ring arrived and I could scrape up the money to fly out there again.

"Good." I rested my elbows on my knees, phone pressed to my right ear as I stared out at the cobalt waves churning under the gray late-afternoon haze. The salty breeze, both humid and cold, bit through me, but Cora's low hum wrapped me in its warm embrace. "I can almost see you."

"Yep. I think I can see you too," she said with a throaty laugh. She had the husky voice of a young blues singer, both ethereal and erotic at the same time. Paired with dark, glossy hair and sage green eyes that doubled as a fucking defibrillator, she was jaw-dropping. A total knockout. And one hundred percent mine.

"How many fingers am I holding up?" I lifted my index finger. This shit never got old for us. A year and some months into our grad school careers, we needed anything that minimized the crushing weight of the distance.

"Two."

I lifted my middle finger to join the index. "Correct."

Her soft laugh floated through me, dispelling all the stress I'd brought from the week. Seconds into our calls, everything in the world felt right. Just as if we were at the beach together.

"You'd tell me I was right even if you didn't have any fingers."

"Well, sweet cheeks, it's because you're always right," I told her. I dropped a hand to the sand, beginning the absent-minded search for sea glass. The other important ritual of our beach visits.

"Not always."

"Well you're right about one thing, at least."

The smirk on her face was evident in her voice. "And what's that?"

"Being with me."

This was the part where I'd wrap her into my arms again and we'd fall back onto the sand and stay there for a long time, possibly until dusk, or until the weird goth guys ran us off with the shitty accordion music (if we were in LA). But I couldn't, and my chest throbbed with the absence of her heat there. Time wasn't making things better or easier. In fact, each additional day away from her only proved how much I didn't want a life without her. We'd spent our third anniversary on opposite coasts, wishing we could tonguefuck each other though FaceTime. I didn't want our fourth to be more of the same. I gathered my jacket tighter around me as a brisk wind whipped down the beach.

"I miss you, Axel."

I could hear the deep well of emotion in her voice. My cheeks twitched, caught between a smile and a grimace. "I miss you more. I'm gonna come out there again soon. Then we can visit that other beach you like to visit. What was it? Glass Beach?"

She sighed contentedly. "You'll love it there. It was a gold mine for Axel-blue glass. When do you think you can come?"

"Once I get paid, I'll buy the ticket." My throat tightened, and I looked down at the fine-grained sand between my bent knees. My internship updating the business plan of a Manhattan-based tech company barely paid the bills. I lived mostly off stock dividends, cryptocurrency funds, and sheer ingenuity. The truth was that I had to finish paying off her ring before I could even hope to afford another plane ticket. "And if that doesn't cover it, I'll hit up Trace."

Cora sighed. "Let me put it on my credit card—"

"No. Your dad will flip if you do that. I don't need him having any more ammo against me."

A heavy silence thudded between us. Her father gathered ammo against me like a doomsday prepper. I needed to convince him to focus on a new delusion, because I was about to piss him off by asking his daughter to marry me. He'd be pissed no matter what—I just needed to make sure that it was more on the side of the fleeting annoyance end of the scale rather than the nuclear meltdown variety.

Cora's dad was the type of man to let his nuclear meltdown spill out and affect society. Killing flora and fauna in its wake, rendering entire landscapes barren and radioactive. The man owned a real estate empire that made sheikhs salivate. He had resources at his disposal that I had only dreamed of. The type of money that led to Cora's actual and profound bewilderment when we started dating and she found out I had a job. *Why on earth would you work during college?* she'd asked me. Her silver spoon naivete was only the first of the million differences between our upbringings.

But the depth of our connection—our love—surpassed all the differences. Even her father's ticking closer and closer to radioactive status didn't matter.

Cora was mine; I was hers. We both knew it, and it didn't matter what he thought.

"I can come back east," Cora blurted after our silence had bled into the rush of waves on our respective coasts.

"He wants you to focus on school." That was the excuse her father always had when she wanted to fly home for a visit. Allan insisted on going to California whenever Cora wanted to see them. The man owned property in Los Angeles, which was where Cora stayed whenever she made the trek from school to Venice Beach. But he also owned Cora's current home in Stanford, as well as untold amounts of other properties anywhere he happened to glance. Cora could stay wherever she damn well pleased, wherever she wanted to go. I knew how to read the subtext. His express goal was to prevent Cora from seeing *me*.

"Axel, I can just buy the ticket. Let him rant and rave. I don't care."

A smile twitched at my lips. I'd always suspected I'd find the best woman in the world to have at my side. I just didn't know she'd be so badass to fling herself face first into a radioactive mess on my behalf.

"You know he's gonna get mad..."

"I don't care. Let him get mad. This long-distance shit is killing me."

My fingers connected with a fragment of beach glass, exactly what I'd been searching for. I picked up the smooth remnant. It gleamed translucent blue in the gray day. "How mad is he gonna be when we start having kids?"

She chuckled softly. Maybe it sounded a little sad. "He'll love them anyway. I know he will."

I studied the pretty sea glass before chucking it away. It wasn't the right one. It needed to be green—a blend of emerald and moss. To match Cora's eyes. I dragged my fingers through the sand again, searching for the next piece. "How mad will he be when we get married?"

My entire body was tense, waiting for her response. She had no idea the ring was in transit. No idea that I planned on asking her within a matter of months, not years. No idea that I physically could not wait any longer than necessary to know that she would be my wife someday.

Her silence felt like an eternity. Finally, she said, "Not mad enough to not come to the wedding."

"You think?" My fingers connected with another piece of sea glass. Clear. I chucked it.

"How could he miss his only living child's wedding?"

She had faith in her old man. I, however, did not. "I'd fucking hope so." My fingers returned to the sand.

"We've got plenty of time for him to come around to all of these ideas," Cora said.

Except we didn't. Not now. Not when my proposal rattled around inside me like energy particles inside the Hadron Collider. This shit was going to burst out of me. Once the ring arrived, it was game over. I'd been stalking the perfect engagement ring for months and had pounced on it like a lion in the fucking Serengeti when I found it, the perfect pear-cut halo twist for my Cora.

The sound of accordion music swelled in the background from Cora's end. I laughed, remembering how weird those artists were the last time I visited Venice Beach. Goth dudes on stilts playing Ariana Grande on a goddamn accordion. I never saw shit like that growing up in the rural outskirts of Louisville. There was a lot of shit I didn't see growing up in rural Kentucky, though. And a few things I wish I'd never seen.

But we'd discovered threads that tied Cora and me up tight like a pair of running shoes. We were both in the "living sibling" category. A designation neither of us ever wanted. But there was one critical difference.

She knew how her brother died. I'd never know where my sister went to or what sort of misery accompanied her to her final days.

"Ooh, I think I found your eyes." Cora's breathy excitement made me perk up. There was always an unacknowledged race to see who could find the other's eye color first in the sea glass. We collected the glass, kept it as an homage to our love. Ten equally beautiful deep moss green pieces were tucked away in the apartment I shared with my brothers. It was one of the few things they didn't know about me, and I liked that Cora got to have a part of me that even my two best friends—my brothers—couldn't access. Cora kept her Axel-blue sea glass in a velvet bag that she hid in her lingerie drawer for no other reason than she thought I'd like to be next to her panties. And trust me, I really did like the Axel-inspired sea glass living with her panties.

"Is it a match?" I asked.

"Yep. I think it is." The smile was evident in her voice. Just then, my fingers connected with another piece. Perfectly emerald moss, with a touch of transparency that made it a shoo-in for adding to my collection.

"I found your eyes too, babe."

She hummed happily. "See? It's God letting us know that distance means nothing when it comes to our love."

I didn't believe in the God part, but I sure believed in the rest of it. "Distance...time...nothing can come between us."

The words felt like an edict, reinforcing the truth so that neither of us forgot it. So that it became a weapon that we both could wield in the war that was sure to unfold soon.

Because no matter how much we loved each other, no matter how close to our MBAs we crept, only one thing truly stood a chance of coming between us.

Allan Margulis and his iron grip on his daughter.

CHAPTER TWO

CORA

Clouds swirl.

Evergreen undertones dance in the air. Axel is near.

His raspy laugh threads through me. The cocksure smile appears above my face. He is lined with cumulonimbus fringe and self-assuredness. The velvet softness of his kisses consumes me.

"Will you marry me?"

Of course I will. I want to say it. My heart is dying to say it. But I can't move my lips. Axel's handsome features are wrought with confusion.

An alarm is ringing, warning me of the decision I have to make.

I jolted up in bed, panic streaking through my veins. The alarm, at least, wasn't a dream. My phone was ringing next to my bed, but Axel wasn't close—he was in New York City. A world away. Too many miles and I felt every single one of them in each breath I took without him near me.

I fumbled to grab the phone, Axel's proposal weighing heavily on me. He hadn't asked me to marry him in real life, but I dreamt almost nightly of his proposal. We just talked about marriage as inevitable. The way our MBAs were inevitable. The way Axel choosing pepperoni pizza above all other varieties was inevitable.

The way my decision regarding the family business was inevitable.

I drew a deep breath when I saw who called: my father. I cleared my throat before I answered, trying to hide the groggy evidence in my voice that I'd fallen asleep after my morning Pilates class.

"Hey, Dad," I said, forcing brightness into my voice.

"Cora Bug." My father's gruff voice was at odds with the pet name. My father always had an agenda, and his word choices weren't exempt. He had so few tender touches for the women in his life that when he employed sweetness, it worked harder for him than any of his employees. "Let's talk schedule."

"Of course." I swung my feet off the bed, heading for my discarded planner in the living room of my condo. The warmth I'd felt from the infrequently used endearment was rapidly fading. "How are you?"

"Let's talk about next weekend."

I flipped to the appropriate pages as the familiar iciness spread across my chest. "Okay."

"You've been offered an exciting opportunity. One you'd be remiss to let slip by."

Exciting for who? My gaze landed on the open blocks of the upcoming weekend. My Friday afternoon mastermind course was the only thing written there. The blank space contained the only constants in my life: *study* and *video chat with Axel.*

"What is it?"

"A partnership, and a path into the future."

The iciness in my chest turned to iron. My eyes fluttered shut. "Let's hear it."

"The board of directors and I have been engaging in the long-range planning for the company. Obviously I can't be CEO forever. And though it's still at least a decade away, I'm thinking about what will happen after my retirement. Of all the available options, there's only one that interests me, and that's with my Cora Bug at the helm."

I was thankful he couldn't see me, since I was sure my face would give away my conflict. I'd been avoiding this conversation since high school. Every day spent at grad school pushed me closer to the point of no return.

Running the family business felt inevitable. My father expected it of me. But I'd quietly avoided the topic for years, declining to give solid answers until I could figure out what made sense.

The only problem was, I wasn't sure when anything was going to make sense. I didn't want to run the business at all. But what I wanted to do—run off with Axel and build a start-up together—was the one thing that my father would almost surely never permit. He wouldn't just look down on it. He would refuse to see it altogether.

"The board and I have decided that it's time to diversify. We've got our eye on a few different industries, but any move I make is going to be with you in mind. This isn't just my legacy. It's your future."

Did I really believe an alternative existed? He'd been planning for my brother to take over the business since Chris was born. Once my brother took his own life, I became the replacement de facto future CEO. The only person he wanted for the job, because his number one pick had committed suicide. How could I step away from that?

But the doubts only increased. I was just biding my time, waiting for an exit plan to become clear. An opportunity that would satisfy my parents *and* my inner desires.

My father went on. "The Rossbergs requested a meeting with the three of us. They're curious about your social innovation course-work at Stanford and I'm curious about their openness to certain business alliances in the future."

His words landed like a hammer. There it was. The agenda on full display. The Rossbergs were one of the only families richer than us on the East Coast. Airline industry moguls with blatant aspirations to cultivate an active space travel program. And the eldest Rossberg son, Eli, was in my MBA program at Stanford. One of many families that commuted between NY and CA.

"You want to merge companies?" The words stuck to my throat. There was no way in hell my father could plan for a merger on this end if he didn't have a bargaining chip. I swallowed hard, studying the blank squares of my weekend. Eli had made it clear that he was interested in me. But I had made it even clearer that I was taken.

"I'd like to merge more than that."

I squeezed my eyes shut. *I'm the bargaining chip.* "Like what?"

"Merge families."

A bitter laugh escaped me. "If you're planning an arranged marriage, just say so."

"Oh, come on. Don't be vulgar. This is the twenty-first century, Cora."

"Right. So what would you call it? In twenty-first century terms."

"This is a business opportunity. One that will translate into a *life* opportunity. That's all it is. You don't need to be so goddamn dramatic."

Tears pricked at my eyes, but they didn't fall. They never fell anymore. I had learned long ago how to school my responses, but even so, the vitriol in his voice tugged me into the past. Back to childhood, when both my brother and I received too many of those verbal slaps to count. I was always *too goddamn dramatic* because I dared show emotion and was quick to cry. My brother had been *too goddamn queer* because he loved theater and had a secret love for all things performance arts. Little did we know then, *emotion* and *creative outlets* had no place in the Margulis dynasty.

"I'm not being dramatic. In fact, I think I'm being rather direct. Tell me what you want from me before I decide whether to go for it."

"This is your decision, Cora. You know I'd never make you do something you don't want to do. I'm just handing you an opportunity to do big things with your life. Like I've always done. Because I'm your father."

My throat tightened, and I looked back at the blank squares. They were the only anchor I had in the tumultuous waters. This was a hurricane that always brewed with my parents. Control under the guise of *helping me out.*

"What happens if I don't want a merger with Eli?" I ask, unable to keep the emotion out of my voice. I didn't even want to mention Axel now, even though my father was more than aware I had a boyfriend.

"I'd say it's too early to make a decision. Why don't you assess all the facts before shutting the door on it? You don't want your emotions to cloud your judgment. Some doors can't be reopened once they're closed."

A familiar cocktail of emotions gripped me. White-hot frustration, alongside an inexpressible rage that simply boiled behind my ribs. A tear escaped my eye, and I wiped it away as though my father could somehow sense it.

"I'll send the meeting details," my father went on, his all-business tone grating against me. "They want to meet in New York this weekend. I'll set the flight plan if you give me the green light."

Excitement prickled to life amid the conflict. "Why New York?"

"They live here, you know that."

"Right, but Eli and I are out west."

"I told you. This is a business opportunity that will translate into a life opportunity. They want the meeting, so we do it on their terms."

I wasn't sure how else I'd get to see Axel any time soon if not for this sanctioned trip. It would save me the hassle of concocting various excuses until I landed on one my father found acceptable.

I didn't *want* to, but…if I agreed to the meeting, I could smother my man with enough kisses to last a few more weeks. We'd missed our third anniversary because of this constant logistical challenge. We had some celebrating to make up for.

"I'll come," I blurted, before I could think better of it.

"You will?" Even my father sounded surprised.

"Yeah." I swallowed a knot in my throat. Seeing Axel for a full night and part of a day was worth suffering through this meeting. I'd figure out how to play the "merger" angle later. After I could tell my boyfriend I loved him in person, and that we'd figure out some way to make our future work. "I'd like the latest flight out on Thursday night, please."

"Excellent. I'll arrange for a driver to pick you up at the airport."

Panic snaked through me as I realized what that meant. If Vince, my father's driver, intersected me at the private jet side of the airport, my chances at escaping to meet with Axel fell to zero. The private jets we used to ferry ourselves back and forth between CA and NY were always available within a few days' notice. But not so much at the last minute.

"Actually, wait," I blurted. "That won't work. Let me check my schedule and I'll figure out the flight plan. I might want to come sooner."

"Won't you miss class?"

"It's group stuff this week, so I have some flexibility." My heart hammered in my chest. I needed to figure out a way to weasel my way into a commercial first-class ticket. That was Plan B, when the private jet schedule didn't jive with our own. My father hated sending me commercial, but I didn't mind. I think he hated the loss of control more than anything. But that was precisely why I needed it for this trip.

"If you wait until Friday, you can attend class *and* make it in time for the meeting," my father said.

But that wouldn't work either. I needed Friday with Axel. No matter what. "I just want to get to New York with time to prepare for the meeting. This is a big deal. A big opportunity." My tongue met dry lips. I prayed he bought the bullshit I fed him. "I'll consult my schedule and figure out some things with my group, and then I can handle the flight plan. Don't worry about it."

I snapped my mouth shut before I could say anything else. Because my father didn't need to hear what rattled around inside my head.

Nothing will prevent me from seeing Axel.

CHAPTER THREE

AXEL

"Are you ever gonna put that thing down?"

Trace paired his words with the condescending eyebrow arch he knew irked me. I squeezed the ring box harder into my palm and sent him the deadliest glare I could muster.

"Are you ever gonna stop being annoying?"

"Are you two ever gonna stop being ridiculous?" Damian intoned from the kitchen, which was barely a separate area in our too-tight-to-breathe Manhattan closet we called a home. Even between three of us, rent was still so expensive that selling an organ wasn't entirely off the table.

"Are you two ever gonna stop asking questions?" I shot back. Silence stretched through the apartment while we all smirked at one another in turn.

"I bet you'll sleep with it under your pillow tonight," Trace finally said.

"Fuck you," I offered, pointing in his direction where he lay on the loveseat, an open textbook on his legs. "I will."

"We should call him the Ring Bearer," Damian muttered as he made a lazy path toward the recliner in our living room. Again, not so much a *room* as a *general area in which all activities occurred.* This place was a step up from our apartment in during our undergrad years at Columbia, though. Back then, we had a bona fide studio apartment, with imaginary walls and a sheet for a bathroom door. Now, we had a two bedroom and took turns sharing the second bedroom every few months. Luxury, only sharing a bedroom with your brothers for half the year.

"Funny," I retorted. "Though I plan to be the groom. Maybe one of you could be the ring bearer?"

My brothers had been giving me shit for approximately a year about this ring purchase. They knew how much it meant to me—but of course no opportunity for ribbing could be ignored between brothers.

"I vote Damian, with his insatiable appetite for human interaction," Trace cracked as Damian settled into the worn brown recliner facing the kitchen. Damian lifted the corner of his lip, his round, wire-rimmed glasses making him look like an early Bill Gates-style nineties computer geek. But with much better hair.

"I'd rather be coding, thanks." When both Trace's and my gazes fell on Damian, he added, "But obviously I'd take a break to go to the wedding."

"You better," I warned him. "But as soon as you start to have a good time, you need to leave. Because no recluse nerd brother of mine can be caught having a good time."

Damian tried to send me a withering look, but a smile ghosted his lips, breaking the façade.

"Depends on where you have it," Damian said, raking a hand through his honey brown tresses. "If you're gunning for a church wedding, I think we can count on nobody having a good time."

Trace kicked Damian in the knee, which elicited a scowl.

"I think the right answer is, 'Brother, I'll have a good time at your wedding no matter where it is,'" Trace corrected.

"I'd fucking hope so," I said, peeking into the box one last time. A constellation of incredibly expensive diamonds winked up at me, sending another jolt of excitement through me. I still didn't have a plan, much less a timeline. Hell, I didn't know if we'd end up having a church wedding. I just knew I was going to ask Cora to marry me the next time I saw her, which probably wouldn't be for a few months.

I had time to plan. And because of that, the proposal would be perfect. I'd settle for nothing less.

My phone buzzed in the deep pocket of my black sweatpants. I knew it was Cora before I even looked at it. My body had a way of alerting me when she called or texted. It was a little weird, but I was never wrong.

"'Sup, cowgirl?" I said into the phone, still looking at the ring. *Cowgirl* was one of my preferred nicknames for her, born from a particularly sweet and sexy trip we'd taken to Kentucky last year. Sweet because she'd met Mama Deb and Papa Gary, and sexy because I'd fucked her senseless in the back acres of my parents' farm under the light of a full moon. She'd been in awe of the sheer ruralness of my parent's house—the wide swaths of hayfields, the rolling horse farms, the way tractors shared the roads with cars. I'd called her cowgirl once while she giggled her way through the chicken coop, and it stuck.

"Oh, that's Cora," Trace said in the same way he always did: a combination groan and announcement.

Cora laughed from the other side of the country. "Hey, babe. Is now a good time?"

"It is. But let me relocate." I headed for my bedroom—I was the lucky one at the moment who didn't have to share. "Fuck you guys," I called over my shoulder before I kicked the door shut. "Now where were we?"

"I think you were about to tell me how much you missed me," she purred into the phone.

I switched the phone to speaker and tossed it on my bed while I got to work selecting the perfect resting spot for the ring box. "It's funny you mention that, because I was just realizing there are no words in the English language to come close to describing that."

"Not one?"

"The ones that exist barely scratch the surface of how much I miss you," I told her while I peered at the shelves of my bookcase. There was too much space there; she could spot it while lounging in my bed. No, this hiding place needed to be rock solid. *Diamond* solid.

"So what are you going to do? Just accept the fate that the English language has handed you?"

I grinned so hard my cheeks hurt. "Babe, I love it when you talk like this."

"Like what?"

"Like one of the judges on *Shark Tank*."

She burst into laughter, and the husky lilt caused both my heart *and* my cock to swell. "We can thank my dad for that."

I didn't want to thank him for anything. A business mogul worthy of joining the cast of *Shark Tank*—that was one of the only good qualities I'd grant the man.

"For that, and for bringing you into the world. But that's about it."

Cora sighed heavily, though I couldn't tell if it transmitted annoyance or agreement. Probably both. "Well, let's not condemn him just yet. He is, after all, putting me on a flight to New York this weekend."

A sputtering noise blocked my airways. My fingers reflexively gripped the ring box while a cough tore through me. "Excuse me?"

"Don't choke and die before I can see you."

"Don't worry, babe. Even if I died, you know I'd haunt you until you came."

That husky laughter thrilled through me again, prompting another grin I couldn't have wiped from my face if I tried.

"God, I love you," Cora said.

"I love you more. So what's the special occasion? Somebody getting married?" I tapped the ring box against my forehead as my brain started sectioning off to conquer the new challenges in front of me. I thought I'd been working with months to plan the perfect proposal. Now she'd be in my arms in mere days, and I wasn't prepared.

But I'd go through with it. So help me God, I was going to ask this woman to marry me when I saw her.

She laughed softly, but it sounded humorless. "Ah...no. Well, I'm sure my father would love if there was a wedding. But no."

"What?"

She started to say something then stopped.

"Cora." I stared at the far wall of the room, where my poster of Elon Musk kept an eternal watch over my belongings. "What does that mean?"

"It means nothing."

"What does that fucking *mean*." I hated when she played coy like this. Her mouth was often faster than her brain, and I could read her like a book. So when she tried to sidestep a comment like that, I had to dig.

When a long sigh ripped out of her, I knew my shovel had struck gold. "He set up a meeting between me and the Rossbergs."

I knew that name—I knew I knew it, in the same way that lesser-cultured people knew the name *Rockefeller* without being entirely sure why. "What for?"

"I don't know. Potential business collaborations, now that Eli and I are graduating soon..."

Eli. The lightbulb went on, but it illuminated a picture I didn't want to fucking look at. "You and Eli, huh?" I knew she and the white-collar bastard went to Stanford together. I'd run into him at a charity function once, one of the few events in their world that Cora's father had allowed her to bring me to. Maybe "allowed" wasn't the right word. I'd slipped in, and I'd been shadow banned ever since. Eli had been a disgusting, smarmy mess—slicked hair, condescension crinkling at his eyes, a sort of bored distaste punctuating his every murmur and movement—even in his mid-twenties.

I remembered this shit because it was so fucking common in the elite circles. My brothers and I even had a bingo card for the most ostentatious signs we were dealing with rich assholes and their ilk. Using the word "ilk" was, ironically, on the bingo card.

"We're in the same program..."

"I know." I squeezed the ring box, a million different questions sprouting to life inside me. The conflicting pressures created a dangerous environment beneath my rib cage. "So the wedding thing—your dad wants you to marry him?"

"I...think so."

A long silence stretched between us, and I felt sick. Of course her dad wanted her to marry Eli. It didn't surprise me. On the list of potential fiancés, anyone with a 401(k) was automatically in line before me. But at the front of the line was anyone who looked, talked, and acted like Eli. Jackpot for coming with family money.

No, what landed like a surprise punch to the balls was the fact that her father was weaving the Rossberg business into Cora's future. This was an opportunity—whatever it was. And I had a sinking suspicion that whatever they wanted to talk about, it would feature a gilded future and lots of cash.

Cora might have a hard time saying *no.*

"So when are you going to tell him the only man you're gonna marry is me?"

She laughed, but it sounded sad. "Well, I guess a good time would be once someone pops the question…"

I ground my teeth, staring at the ring box in my hand. Did she know? Could she *feel* me holding this engagement ring? I tried to keep the amusement out of my voice, lest anything give me away. "Seriously, Cora. When is he going to accept that we're together?"

"I don't know. Once you get your MBA? After your first million? You know, you could fast track it and just go work for him."

A bitter laugh tumbled out of me, one that I couldn't control. "Cora, I love you, but—"

"But what?" The acid edge in her voice told me we were entering new territory here. We never talked about me working for Allan, because it was an idea that could not exist in the real world. Much like dinosaurs would never reincarnate wearing Chuck Taylor shoes and playing the White Stripes, I would never spend a single moment of my life as Allan's subordinate bitch.

"There are other options," I hurried to add. I didn't want to say *but I don't love you that much*, because it wasn't true. When it came down to it, I'd do anything to make Cora mine. No matter how much I postured, I knew that spending time as Allan's subordinate bitch was a possibility, but only if it was the last option.

I'd simply make sure that outcome never arrived.

When she stayed silent longer than I liked, I added, "My brothers and I are starting our business. Like we've been planning for years. Trace already has a lead on some potential clients, and if we can get ten clients right out of the gate, I'll make sure that ten turns into twenty. Twenty into fifty. Fifty into one hundred. And pretty soon your dad will be knocking on *my* door to manage his money."

"I know. I believe in your business. But you know there are other routes that won't...take so long."

I felt my hackles rise. I was used to the entire fucking world doubting me, but not my Cora. "Take so long, huh?"

"Starting a new business takes time. It takes capital."

"No fucking shit."

"Don't snap at me like that, Axel. I'm just being realistic. You're the one who asked me what it would take. Well, I told you."

I squeezed the ring box again, the anxiety churning alongside the frustration. "I didn't mean to be like that. *He* pisses me off—not you."

She laughed so softly it sounded like a sigh. "I know, babe. And I believe in your business. I support it. But you can do other things before you become a millionaire."

I popped open the black velvet box, looking at the brilliant diamonds floating over the gold band. Maybe she was right. Maybe the only way to get this ring on her finger was to suck it up and become Allan's subordinate bitch.

She navigated the conversation to safer topics: schoolwork, funny stories from the day, memories from the last time I'd made her come. We talked until her next class started, and then I was left staring at Elon Musk, clutching the velvet ring box harder than if I expected Allan to come in here and rip it from my hands.

"Guys." I pushed the door to my bedroom, beelining for my brothers. "You got a minute?" The conversation with Cora rattled through me, like the warning shake of a warlock's skull-topped walking stick. This needed to be addressed. If it wasn't, secret poison might take root and I'd decay from the inside out.

"What's up?" Trace looked up from his book; Damian pushed his laptop aside wordlessly, the strongest signal he knew how to give that he was listening.

"You'd tell me if proposing to Cora was a bad idea, right?" I still clutched the ring box. I might never let it go. "With how her dad feels about us and everything."

Inscrutable looks settled on their faces. And I didn't like that shit one bit.

"I was just talking to Cora, and she brought up the idea that I might need to go work for Allan in order to...you know..."

"Get a yes?" Trace finished for me.

"Cora will say yes whether I work for her father or not," I said.

"I mean get a yes from *him*," Trace clarified.

I sent him a withering smile. "I'm not asking for his blessing."

"Why not?" Damian asked.

"Yeah, you probably could stand to get into his good graces," Trace said, tossing his book on the lopsided coffee table.

"If I ask for his blessing, he'll tell me no. Besides, posturing wouldn't get me into his good graces. It just tells him his opinion matters, which it doesn't."

Silence stretched across the living room, the first sign my brothers didn't agree with me. They'd developed this annoying habit over the years. When I'd rather they would come out and fight me about it, they let me simmer in my own doubts and discontent first.

I always cracked first. "What?"

Trace narrowed his eyes. "Bro, you need to posture for this one."

"Why bother?"

"Why wouldn't you?" Damian shot back. The *duh* tone in his voice made me angle toward him.

"I don't want to waste time asking for the blessing of a man who will barely sneeze in my direction. I thought you both understood that."

"Yeah, we do," Trace said with the type of cocky look that annoyed the fuck out of me, "but that was before you planned to marry his daughter. This guy could do a thousand different things to make your life harder, any day of the week. You could play by his rules for once and make your life a little easier."

"Fuck his rules." I squeezed the ring box again, as though testing it was still there. Testing that this dream of mine—*make Cora my wife*—was still alive.

"That's what you always say," Damian said.

"And I always mean it. Fuck his rules."

Damian rolled his eyes. "You come out here asking if proposing is a bad idea and then get pissy when we tell you the truth."

I blinked rapidly, turning so my entire body faced Damian. So I could pounce if needed. "Excuse me? Were you looking to get beaten up in the middle of your little coding assignment?"

Laughter escaped him, and he let his head fall back on the couch. "Jesus, Axel. Excuse me for answering your question."

"You don't have to be a fucking dick about it," I shot back. Tension burbled in the air between the three of us while I mulled over their words. They had a point—one I didn't want to admit out loud. So I followed up with, "So let's say, in an alternate universe, you guys have a point."

"In an alternate universe," Trace repeated.

"I'd go meet up with him and what? Ask for his daughter's hand in marriage? I'd feel like I'm about to board the Titanic or something."

"You want to prove to him that you are *not* a bad idea," Damian said. "Right? Well, how do you do that? You need to tell him what your direction is. What *our* direction is."

"Yeah," Trace added, "Tell him about our business. Make him feel like you're not driving blind. Convince him your future is solid and that he can rest assured his daughter's future is equally secure."

"Show him the fucking business plan," Damian added.

"The business plan?" It wasn't done. Not by a long shot. I had four different iterations going with wildly varying projections. Trace and I couldn't settle on the ideal profit margin. I shot for the stars, while he wanted to be *conservative* and shot for the tree line.

But I didn't play like that. Not when my future was at stake. It was go big or go bury your fucking head in the sand. I didn't particularly like the taste of sand in my teeth, so I knew where we were headed.

"We've got enough drawn up that we could start hunting for investors," Trace said. "Even though we're not finalized, I think we're ready enough to prove that you're serious."

"I haven't even started the LLC," I told him. "This motherfucker will be the first to shoot me down because my paperwork isn't in order."

"It's not like he's gonna check your tax ID number," Damian muttered.

"You don't think he will? He probably runs a monthly background check on my ass just for fun."

Trace shrugged. "You want to go to that pitch unprepared, then do it. But if this is how the CEO of Fairchild Enterprises works, then maybe we need to talk."

"Oh my g—Trace. You are fucking ruthless." I wasn't sure if I was more upset or amazed by his boldness. Questioning my commitment to our business, right to my face. What an asshole. A brilliant asshole. "You're gonna be the next one I pound into the couch."

He looked pleased with himself. "Maybe *I* should be the CEO."

"Absolutely not. You have no idea how to woo the pants off people. You should stick to cold hard cash."

"You haven't wooed Cora's dad," Damian pointed out.

"Thank you, Damian, for your overstatement of the obvious." I kneeled on the couch so I could punch him in the shoulder, which he accepted with a muffled laugh. "That man barely likes his own family. I never had a chance. So it's a moot point."

"Great. So it's settled. You'll stop letting your emotion cloud your judgment," Trace said, adding a smirk at the end that told me how much pleasure he derived from calling me out like this.

"I've had about enough from your smartass mouth," I said, closing the gap between us so that I could deliver a blow to his shoulder as well. He just laughed, because he knew he was right. Hell, even I knew he was right.

If this weren't about the one person I loved more than life itself, I'd have no problem waltzing into her father's office and putting it all on the line.

Cora was the one thing in my life I couldn't stand to lose. I couldn't gamble with her. I would accept no negative response to the big question.

But I had to treat this like another of the chameleon social moments I'd gotten so good at over the years. If this were a business deal, Trace was right—I'd be posturing the fuck out of this.

I ground my teeth as I played with the idea. I could already see it, however much I didn't want to—meeting Allan on his turf somewhere. Sharing my meticulously crafted business plans. Telling him how much Cora meant to me. Practically getting down on one knee to propose to him too.

My brothers were right. They knew it. And they knew that I knew it, too.

I finally slipped the ring box into the right pocket of my sweats.

"You'll both be my best men, right?" I asked.

I got two cocky smiles in return.

CHAPTER FOUR

CORA

AXEL: You're close, aren't you?
AXEL: Never mind.
AXEL: I can smell you. You're here.

I grinned down at my phone as the text messages rolled in. The five-hour first-class flight from LAX to JFK on airplane mode had been a nice pause on life. And now, as I drifted untethered through the throngs of people in the airport, I realized this was true luxury. My father wasn't breathing down my neck for once. I'd managed to swindle my way into booking the flight home with our travel agent all by myself. And now that I was in New York proper, all I could think about was Axel. What he might taste like once I kissed him. How good he'd smell as he wrapped his arms around me.

It had been three months since we'd last seen each other—back in August, during one of my visits home from Stanford. We'd only gotten two days together, since my father made a habit of over-scheduling my visits home. But we'd crammed in enough love and tenderness to last us these months apart and more.

Even though Axel was my true love—the one man I could be my true self with—my stomach was in knots imagining how it would be to see him again. Three months was both nothing and everything.

Doubts crept in no matter what I did to bat them away. Maybe he wouldn't like what he saw…maybe I acted differently now after so much time away and didn't even realize it. Doubt and insecurity circled like a predator while I speed walked through JFK, clutching my rolling luggage behind me.

DAD: Got your flight details from the agent. Vince is waiting for you. See you soon.

Fuck. The doubts and insecurities from before began churning, hissing bubbles as they fermented into something new altogether. A familiar paralysis that spread through my veins like ice and iron at the same time. Weighing me down, trapping me. My father loved to orchestrate everything. The car. The destination. The time. My entire fucking life.

I fired off a quick text to Axel letting him know I'd landed, and then slipped my phone into my oversized Dior purse. It was just after seven p.m., darkness creeping at the edges of the earth despite the bright haze of activity emanating from the airport. This night would be mine. No matter what my father thought.

I strode quickly through the crowded terminal, my black rolling luggage a perfect companion to the Hermes bag hanging from the crook of my elbow. My parents formed me in their image, and that image included expensive accessories, picture-perfect hair at all times, and a take-no-shit attitude in negotiations. Nothing else mattered. Not to them, at least. They wanted the finest things in life, with the finest looking people, at the most favorable rates possible. That was it.

Which meant that Axel loved giving me shit about the accessories. I could already *feel* him ribbing me about the Hermes bag, which was less my choice and more of a requirement for the upcoming meeting this weekend. I knew this—it was just part of the life that I lived. I couldn't show up to a meeting with Eli's parents carrying the teal handstitched cross-body bag I'd bought on the Venice board-walk last spring, even if it was my favorite accessory. I needed to bring the items that fit the persona they expected from me. Starting with this $25,000 French handbag.

I knew that my late brother, Chris, would have preferred the teal cross-body bag too. I'd heard his voice in my head when I bought it, which had made me cry into Axel's shoulder for fifteen minutes in broad daylight.

No. This huge, disgustingly glamorous bag was considered an oc-cupational obligation. With a few other choice four-figure-price-tag items that I had tucked away in my rolling luggage, like the Chanel laptop case and the 24K gold USB drive. These were items I knew I needed. For *them*. Not for me. None of these things were items I would have picked if I weren't trying to create the image *they* wanted for me.

The closer I got to baggage claim, the closer I got to Axel. I imag-ined he'd be waiting just outside the automatic doors of baggage claim, maybe backed up against the long string of cars that dotted the inner belt of JFK like dirty pearls. I was five steps into baggage claim when my forearms went prickly. Excitement swirled in my chest, so intense I was already breathless. All I could focus on was the sliding doors leading out into the world. My heels clicked against the tile of the floor, wheels of my luggage clacking in time. *Axel Axel Axel.*

A strong arm caught me around the ribs. I didn't even have time to gasp, or even blink, but my body knew what had happened before my brain did.

"There you are."

Axel's gruff bass traveled through my body like an electrical cur-rent. Every inch of me understood his touch, the solid warmth of him as he gathered me against him. I wasn't sure if I said anything or if my shock—or maybe my relief—had rendered me mute. My face was against the flat plane of his chest, buried into the sweatshirt he wore beneath his trademark—if battered—black leather jacket.

His arms squeezed around me, locking me against him. Tears pricked at the corner of my eyes as I melted into him, clutching him wherever I could grab—the side of his jacket, the waist of his jeans.

"Jesus, Axel," I blubbered into his chest, heart racing like I'd run a marathon. The hug couldn't go on long enough. I could hug him until three a.m. and still want more.

He pressed kisses to the top of my head as I drank him in with my senses—the ropy muscle of his arms around me, the outdoors-and-cedar scent of him, as if he carried the woods of Kentucky with him wherever he went.

When his grip around me loosened, I pushed onto my tiptoes, my lips seeking his like two parts of a magnet coming together. Our mouths smashed together, too urgent and greedy for a delicate peck. His hand snaked up the back of my neck, fingers knotting in my hair at the base of my skull. I whimpered through the kiss while he tugged at my hair slowly, gently. Exactly as I liked it. Moisture surged between my legs. Axel knew all my secret spots and loved to tease them. Even in the middle of JFK baggage claim.

"I'm gonna eat you alive, sweet cheeks," he promised, his lips still pressed to mine. His mouth curled at the corners, and he lifted me off the ground, twirling me in a circle.

"Promise?"

"Promised and notarized."

I nuzzled him, giggling as he set me back down. But his arms didn't leave me. I tilted my head to really look at him, drink in all the changes and minute differences since I'd seen him last. His dirty blond hair was longer at the top, disheveled in a way that I wanted to protect. The stubble on his jawline scraped at my fingers as I stroked him, trying to memorize every detail about this moment.

"Get a fucking room," someone muttered as they walked past. Axel and I stared at each other with big smiles for a moment before bursting into laughter.

"I would if I could afford it," Axel shouted in the general direction of the person who'd scolded us. "This city is so expensive, you have no idea!"

I collapsed against him, laughter shaking my body.

"Good thing we only need a closet," Axel went on, pressing a kiss to my forehead. "Because you know that's what I got for ya."

"It's my favorite closet in Manhattan," I told him, eyes drifting shut as he placed another kiss to my lips. The kind that was crushed velvet and heat. The kind that made panties smolder.

"You ready to go cuddle up by my shoe rack?" His eyes twinkled as he teased me, his palm smoothing over my hair. I loved being admired by him—nobody else in the world had ever looked so genuinely and deeply elated to see me.

I opened my mouth to tell him that my dad had snooped my flight plan and sent the driver, but being around Axel again emboldened me. Let the consequences pile up as they may. I needed to spend the night at my boyfriend's house, and if that included telling Vince to fuck off, so be it.

"Of course I am." I slung my arms around his neck, and we kissed again. And then again. When we broke apart, I spotted my father's driver Vince over Axel's shoulder. My stomach pitched to my feet.

"Let's go to the other side of baggage claim," I said softly. "Vince just showed up, probably to find me and steal me away."

Annoyance flashed across Axel's face, but he must have squashed it because he scooped my hand into his and brought the back of my hand to his lips.

"Time to start the kidnapping," he said.

I followed Axel's lead, and we scurried away, easily getting lost among the throngs of people crossing through baggage claim. All I wanted was for us to escape for a long weekend—head to a cabin, snuggle up in some blankets, stare at a fire for days. But given my current circumstances, the weekend getaway was impossible. This would have to do—a stolen night here, a renegade brunch in two days if we were lucky. And then...more waiting.

Waiting, waiting, waiting until we could steal another night. Until my father stepped down as the main obstacle between us. Until the stars finally aligned so that we could be openly happy together. Making plans without friction and secrecy. God willing, we might even be able to wake up and go to sleep in the same house someday. It was a reality I could almost taste but had no road map for how to arrive there.

We got lost in the stream of pedestrians as Axel guided me back into the airport, up toward departures. Every step at his side felt like an adventure—it had since the day I met him, in line at the student union waiting for a mid-day grilled cheese with a slice of pepperoni stuck in the middle, and he'd asked if I wanted to ditch class and go to Chinatown with our grilled cheeses. He'd been a total stranger, but something about the mischief and innocence in his gaze had made me answer yes. And I'd been answering yes ever since.

"You've got the fancy purse today, I see," he murmured as we maneuvered through the crowds.

"I have the Venice Beach bag along too."

"Good. It brings Chris with you, you know?"

I smiled. Axel wasn't afraid to talk about Chris. Not like everyone else was. My parents had only mentioned him a handful of times since he'd taken his life six years ago.

"You know, every time I wear that bag, I can hear his laugh in my head. I think he was with us that day on the beach."

"That shit happens to me with Jordan and Kaylee," he said, smiling warmly at me. He'd lost his two younger sisters—victims of the foster care system. Kaylee had passed away the brothers' freshman year of college. Jordan had simply disappeared, and though the brothers still held out a flicker of hope, they told themselves she'd suffered a similar fate as Kaylee. The same system that took his sisters had allowed him and his biological brother Damian to flourish. "Sometimes I just swear they're hanging out with me for a day."

I laughed. "Maybe they just pop in from Heaven to visit."

"It's like the spirit version of Bring Your Kid to Work Day, except—" he glanced at me, probably reading the confusion on my face. "No, Margulis Realty didn't do Take Your Kid to Work Day, did they?"

"They did not," I said with a laugh.

"You didn't miss much," he mused.

But our lost siblings were still heavy on my mind as we moved through the airport. "Do you ever beat yourself up trying to still honor their memory?"

Axel let a low whoosh of air go. But not because this was too heavy. This was just how we were—we could talk about it all. Whenever and wherever. He was the first person I could just let it all out with.

"Every fucking day," he confirmed. "Damian too."

"I feel like there's so much I have to do to make things right," I murmured. These were words I had never—could never—utter around my parents. They viewed Chris taking his own life as an act so heinous and embarrassing that they refused to speak about it. Even with me.

"Sounds like you need some TLC, babe. I don't know if I'm gonna let you go this time," Axel said, squeezing his arm around my shoulders as we weaved through the crowds. "Your MBA isn't that big of a deal, right? You'll be fine if I lock you up in my apartment."

"Yeah. As long as you feed and water me. I wouldn't even be considered a victim."

"Because you'd be willing." The sexy smirk that stretched across his face as he looked down at me had the power to turn this joke into reality. Because I'd do anything for him. Including sabotage my career, if necessary.

Including forsake my family...if necessary.

"We can just share your MBA," I cracked, as a gust of the chilly wind whipped past. I burrowed deeper into his embrace.

"You can have it," he said. "I'm only getting it for you anyway."

I laughed and swatted at his chest, but he didn't return my laughter. "You aren't serious."

A shrouded look crossed his face. "I know it'll look better to your dad if I have my MBA. And it'll look better for the CEO of our business to have an MBA. But after the week I've had, I'm ready to fucking drop out."

I patted his chest. "We're almost through it. Because you're right. It will look better to have it. You've come this far. Why stop now?"

He grunted in the most Axel-like fashion, a mix between a petulant adolescent and a bull. "Because I'm over it."

"You're more than halfway through—"

"And more than halfway broke. Trace is graduating this semester, which means we can get a jump on the business. And we need to. Besides, I was ready two years ago to be CEO; so why flush all this extra money down the drain just to receive the bragging rights of a Colombia MBA?" He sighed, the blue thunderstorm of his gaze darting over the crowds. "I'm so conflicted. Trapped between money and commitment yet again."

"Axel, if there's anyone who can figure out a solution to this problem, it's you."

"I'm sick of having to always figure out the solution." His throat bobbed as he gazed off into the distance. "I've been dealing with this shit my whole life. I just thought that once I got to this point, it would get easier."

A sad laugh floated out of me. I could relate to that statement in about a hundred different ways. "It doesn't get easier. You just get used to it."

Axel squeezed his arm tighter around my shoulders. "I didn't want to start our night with all my bitching. Will you forgive me?"

I grinned up at him. "Hmmm. I suppose there is a way you could make it up to me."

That heartbreaker smile returned to his face—the type of look that held me hostage whenever he directed this brilliance my way. The type of smile I'd see even when I was dead. "Can I start making it up to you now?"

I couldn't respond before he scooped me up into his arms with a whoop. I clung to him, giggling and delirious with joy. I was no stranger to the random public displays of affection that Axel loved to put on, yet they never failed to delight. My rolling luggage was forgotten as he tossed me over his shoulder, patting my ass like this might help me stay in place.

"There we go," he said. *Loudly*. "Right where I like ya."

Laughter cascaded out of me. "Oh my god, Axel. Put me down." People streamed by us, barely registering the ripple in the space-time continuum of the walkway.

"I'm making it up to you. You get to stare at my ass for the next hundred yards. There's no greater gift, babe."

I couldn't even talk for how hard I was laughing. His arrogance was only preceded by his humor. This type of bawdy display would earn us plenty of stern looks and even a vicious dressing-down from my mother if this were happening anywhere near them. But that was one of the things I loved about my boyfriend.

He didn't give a fuck about the rules of my world.

And I loved flying free in his.

An hour later, we stumbled up the steps of his walk-up, barely able to focus on walking between all the kisses and laughter. I'd laughed more in the past hour with him than I had in the previous two months without him. Further proof that my sanity and well-being *required* Axel in my life.

He fumbled with the lock on the door, trying and failing to insert the key.

"Come on, babe." I snagged his lips in another kiss, tugging at the buckle of his belt.

He drew in a sharp breath, sending me a warning look. Heat pooled in his slate blue gaze, a promise of the passions lurking inside him, waiting to explode the second we got behind the closed door of his bedroom. "Cora…"

"What?"

He stilled, his throat bobbing. Emotion crowded out the heat in his gaze, the entire world around us disappearing until only this moment remained. "I love you, you know that?"

"Of course I know that. I love you too."

He smashed his lips against mine, a kiss both desperate and hungry. When we broke apart, my lips tingling and entire body electrified, he finally managed to insert the key.

"There we go," he said as it swung open.

"I was about to call the cops," someone deadpanned from inside. Damian. He leaned his head back from his position on the couch, laptop in front of him as always.

"For what? Breaking and not entering?" Axel teased, his grip tight around my hand as we came inside. I smiled brightly at Damian, waving with the tips of my fingers.

"Long time no see, Damian."

"Glad you made it back to our neck of the woods," Damian said with an imaginary hat tip.

"Couldn't keep me away."

Axel shot me a mysterious look. Trace emerged from the hallway a moment later, a reassuring smile at the ready.

"There's Cora," he said as he came my way to wrap me in a side-hug. "The only woman who Axel looks at, thinks about, or talks about."

"That's enough chitchat, guys," Axel said. His grip around my hand tightened, and he beelined for the bedroom door. "Got some things to do. See you tomorrow."

Axel tugged me behind him, and I offered a helpless smile to his brothers. As we stepped into his room, I heard Trace laugh and say, "*Right.* Things to do."

The door clicked shut. The muffled undertones of Trace and Damian's conversation outside faded away as Axel gripped my arms, pinning me with a look that promised he'd devour me.

But instead of kissing me, his throat bobbed. "Cora."

"What, babe?"

His gaze fell, and he sank to his knees in front of me, his palms tracing slow, intentional lines down the sides of my body. Every inch of me went electric beneath his grip. He didn't normally waste time when we were alone together. And getting down onto his knees...was he finally going to pop the big question? He'd been hinting at it for over six months. Butterflies swarmed my belly as I waited for him to finally make good on the hinting.

But he didn't say anything, just kept me pinned against the door with his gaze. His hands converged on the mound of my pussy, which was covered by my expensive leggings. His thumb slipped into the hot groove between my legs. I hadn't worn panties—for him—but he was so good at weaponizing my own thoughtfulness. What was supposed to be a sexy surprise for him would now become my own unraveling. He dragged his thumb in a slow circle, and I arched toward him.

"I can't believe you're here," he finally said, curling his fingers around my hip. His thumb pressed in just the right spot against the fabric of my leggings. My breath hitched.

"Oh my God, Cora." He dragged his thumb back and forth over the tight peak of my clit, which he could probably feel though my leggings, from how turned on I was. "You're not wearing any panties, are you?"

A weak laugh slipped out of me. My head dropped back to the door. "How could you tell?"

"Because you're always so sweet like that." He wet his bottom lip and tugged at my leggings, jerking them down to my knees in one practiced swoop. His jaw flexed as he looked at my bare pussy head-on.

"Spread your legs."

He never wasted time. I loved this about him. But the leggings bunched at my knees didn't allow for a lot of give. "Babe, I can't—"

"There we go." The corner of his mouth lifted as my legs parted just a couple of inches. And then he dove forward, mouth to mound, burying his tongue between the lips of my pussy. His tongue found my clit first, eager and expectant, the warm heat feeling like both an old friend and the newest, most amazing sensation in the world. A moan began to escape, but I cut it off—his brothers were outside. Not like they couldn't imagine what our first order of business was.

Axel made a muffled, sloppy noise. I was embarrassingly wet. It was always this way with him.

"Jesus, Axel," I breathed, running my fingers through the messy length of his hair. I knotted my fingers in the strands while his tongue assaulted my clit. To ground myself and because I knew he loved it. He grunted, plunging his tongue into my slit with abandon. I arched harder against him, welcoming more. Axel snaked his fingers between my legs, pumping two fingers in and out of me slowly.

"You're dripping." He pulled back to look at me, his face shining with my juices. His heated gaze dragged up my body, then back to my pussy. "Jesus, you're a fucking dream."

A lazy smile drifted across my face, but it faded quickly when his thick fingers filled me again. He sucked at my clit, my head thudding against the door from the jolt of pleasure. I moaned again, but this time I couldn't stop it. Axel worked his tongue mercilessly back and forth against the peak of my clit. The impossible bliss began a slow uncoiling inside me, sending out exploratory paths of heat and pinpricks through my entire body.

"Ohhhh, Axel. I'm close." I thrust my hips against him, the pleasure rising to a rapid crescendo. When he eased his fingers deeper inside me, he sucked hard at my clit, and all the walls came tumbling down. Knees to jelly. Fireworks. Heat pummeling me, perfect bliss from head to toe. I slumped but he caught me, the door banging behind me as he propped me up.

From the living room, Trace and Damian were mocking us. "Oh, Axel!" Trace mimicked in a falsetto.

Giggles floated out of me. I couldn't even open my eyes.

Axel's rough voice brought me back to earth, the barely-there Kentucky accent making me melt further. "You okay, babe?"

I laughed and laughed. I was more than okay. I was perfectly happy in this moment.

And I knew it, because I spent every other moment of my life *not* happy.

I needed to hang on to this bliss for as long as I could.

Because the clock was ticking until real life set in again. As soon as I stepped outside the door of this apartment, the honeymoon was over.

CHAPTER FIVE

AXEL

My breath came out in a single white puff in front of me. New York was extra frigid today, though it might have been because I was about to enter the front doors of Margulis Realty. Cora had left my apartment that morning, and I could still taste her kisses on my lips. I felt both dreamy and reckless, like Romeo before he pulled all that crazy shit with Juliet's family. Which was probably why I was here in the first place.

I knew a guy who worked for Allan. Entry level, but he was on the inside. Jake and I had gone to undergrad at Columbia together. I gave him $10 grand after we had our first windfall from when Trace squeezed Wall Street. He'd needed it to cover his mom's funeral costs, and we've been linked ever since. There's something about helping a guy pay for a funeral, I guess. I hadn't planned on calling in a favor until Jake mentioned he worked on the bottom rung of Allan's company. He knew the right people to get me on Allan's schedule—under an alias, of course.

Just call me Spencer Wattford.

The inside of the building was slick and gray, like polished steel had sex with marble. Smackdab in the middle of the foyer was a ginormous glass sculpture, curling up out of the floor like tendrils of smoke. It was equal parts gaudy and fascinating—even though my first thought was that the sculpture represented the flames of the souls Allan burned in order to stay on his golden perch.

The air itself was blanketed with hushes, though I wasn't sure if people were too afraid of Allan to make noise or if it came from reverence of the real estate industry. Allan's company moving into this building had been a big deal in the early 2000s, apparently—not like I was in NYC then, or cared about his business, but Cora had told me the inaugural party here was one of her earlier memories—and well-documented in *Time* magazine.

And I guess, in a way, I could see it. The place was both cavernous and professional, artistic yet tasteful. But every last inch of it screamed money. The walls themselves were woven with the memories of the Caribbean vacations the Margulis family had taken so frequently Cora had viewed the Cayman Islands as her backyard as a child. The floor was polished with the millions of dollars of interest her father's investments made in his sleep. The air itself pressed down on all corners with the immense weight of his wealth.

Don't fucking freak yourself out. I jabbed at the silver dollar of an Up button at the elevator, my gaze wandering to the worn sleeves of my leather jacket. It was a stark contrast to the rest of my outfit—pressed navy pants, a crisp white button-up. But I didn't own a formal coat.

I slid my leather jacket off, my gaze bouncing around the lobby. I knew I couldn't go into the meeting with this sad, beat-up excuse for a jacket. Not that I'd ever say those things in front of it—I loved my jacket. It just couldn't accompany me upstairs. I spied an ostentatiously large fern nearby—something like Jurassic Park foliage on steroids. Seemed like a good enough coat check for now. I folded my jacket as small as it would go and tucked it among the fronds. It would be there when I came back—I knew it. Nobody who came to this building would ever need to steal a shitty jacket from inside a fern.

The doors of the elevator slid open and I stepped inside, my likeness reflected back to me endlessly through the walls lined in mirrors. It was easy to get lost in the trappings of wealth—that was something I'd learned immediately at Columbia and at every soiree I attended with Cora. And it was when you got lost in the trappings that made it so easy for them take the upper hand.

But I wasn't going to be distracted by the glitz and the marble. I might hide my jacket in his damn fern, but Allan wasn't going to win. This whole display of wealth wasn't going to distract or intimidate me. I'd calmly and firmly approach Allan about my unwavering intent to marry his daughter. Hell, I'd even invite him to the wedding. I was a nice guy, after all.

When the doors slid open, the emotionless face of a receptionist greeted me.

"Spencer Wattford," I said in lieu of a greeting, affecting the same disinterested energy she doled out. You had to play the game in this world. I knew how to play the game. I wet my bottom lip and attempted a casual lean on her desk. "I'm here to meet with Mr. Margulis."

Her gaze raked over me, prickly and disapproving. She consulted her computer, assessed me once more as though searching for my name tag. I knew better than to reiterate my identity. Reiteration was a sure mark of lying, or worse, desperation. Again, part of the game in this world. Lying was fine, but to be seen as desperate? There was no graver sin. I remained steadfast, my cool smile unwavering. As long as nothing about me betrayed the hammer of my heart, I was fine.

"One moment please." She frowned, her nails clicking against her keyboard as she typed out something. Then she sighed, dragging her disapproving look my way once more. "He'll see you."

The receptionist led me down the long hallway. Through the windows, dusk tugged at the edges of daylight, impatient and sultry. Manhattan stretched like metal clockwork away from our fortieth-floor perch. At the end of the hallway, the receptionist knocked twice, waited for something, and then pushed the door open. She pinned me with a dead stare.

"Good luck."

I mustered a smile and brushed past her, fighting the urge to return with snark. The office of Allan Margulis spread luxuriously around me. Two entire walls were floor to ceiling windows with the best view of New York City I'd ever seen. Unobstructed New York City. Photographers probably paid big bucks for *this* exact view. And this was Allan's ho-hum everyday landscape.

"Mr. Margulis." I forced my gaze off the glittering anthill of life beyond the windowpanes. "Great to see you again."

Allan sat behind an enormous desk, a laptop pushed off to the side, papers stacked neatly into color-coded letter trays. His dark hair was immaculately arranged, in a constant state of Ken doll. He was a bear stuffed into an Armani suit, the same business casual shade of navy as mine, but probably sixty thousand dollars more expensive. He looked up at me, brows beginning a slow trek toward the center of his face.

"What the fuck are you doing here?" Clarity sharpened his sage green eyes, the same hue as Cora's but far more threatening.

"I set up an appointment with your office," I said, donning my best neutral voice. I had to erase any hint of *duh* from my voice, because this man was .05 seconds away from kicking me out already.

He snatched up his cell phone from his desk with the practiced swipe of a jaguar. He checked something, then looked up at me. "So when did you legally change your name to Spencer Wattford?"

"Today." Oops. Snark had a way of slipping out sometimes.

"Get out."

"Allan, please." I held up my palms, as if this might convince him of my harmlessness. "I only need five minutes of your time. Your receptionist blocked you off for thirty minutes with Spence. This is a win-win, because then you'll be ahead of schedule."

His jaw flexed and his blue stare turned cloudy; a storm was rolling in. "You have *one* minute. Starting now."

"Great. I work best under pressure." I stuffed my hands in my pockets, running my tongue back and forth inside my cheek as I struggled to remember the monologue I'd prepared. But all I could think was *fuck you*, which wasn't helpful. I needed to both calm myself down *and* get him to loosen up slightly. Maybe offering him a Xanax first would get the ball rolling.

"Thank you," I started, my heart hammering so loudly I wondered if he could hear it. "Your office is absolutely stunning. I've never seen a view as amazing as this." I gestured unhelpfully to Manhattan through the window. "Honestly, this sort of thing is a goal for me—"

"Get to the point."

I swallowed hard. "Right. You're probably aware that your daughter and I are, uh..." All words failed me. I swiped my tongue across my bottom lip. This man was going to fucking murder me up here, and his receptionist would cover for him. If I made it out alive, I was marrying Cora straight away. "We've been together for a long time now. And I wanted to formally just, uh, you know—"

"Forget how to speak?"

I cleared my throat. The man wasn't known as a shark for nothing. "I plan to ask Cora to marry me." My neck went hot as Allan's face went from snide to blank. Somehow, the emotion draining out of him was scarier than any other reaction I'd imagined. "I thought you should know. And I want to see what we can do to make this relationship between us a bit more...pleasant."

He stared at me, but he'd checked out. He stared so long that the last thread of my ultra-faked cool exterior was fraying. *Say something, already.* I rubbed at the back of my neck, but I wouldn't crack first. The silence became deafening. When he finally blinked, it at least let me know that I hadn't killed him on the spot with the news.

"You actually think she's serious about you?"

The words landed like an uppercut. I swallowed the pain. "I know she is."

"You're batshit crazy if you think she'll marry you."

I stuffed my hands back into my pockets, reminding myself to bite my tongue. There was one batshit crazy person in this room, but I didn't want to tell Allan it was him. "She and I have already discussed the future. I know she'll accept when I ask. I wanted to extend the courtesy of—"

"The courtesy." Snide laughter rolled out of him, and he pushed to standing, palms propped against the desk. "Now that's fucking hilarious."

"I'm not joking, Allan." I swallowed, thinking better of using his name so casually. "Sir."

"Don't you fucking *sir* me. You haven't had an ounce of respect for me or my family since the day you met Cora. It's not just laughable that you're in my office, disrespecting me yet again by giving falsified information to my staff, it's reprehensible. And then you have the gall to tell me you're marrying my daughter?" His body shook with bitter laughter. "Absolutely fucking ridiculous."

I squeezed my hands into fists. It wasn't going exactly what I would call *well*. "If I'd given my real name, you never would have let me through the door."

"And with good reason!" He slammed his palm against his desktop, causing some papers to flutter to the ground. "You lie to get through the door, what else will you lie about? Your income? Your stability? Can't trust a fucking word you say, boy. My daughter deserves more than that. She deserves someone at her level, in every sense—which will never be you."

My throat tightened, and I straightened my back. "I'm just over six months away from securing my MBA. I have an LLC start-ed"—A slight white lie, but now was not the time to retreat; I needed to go balls to the wall—"and my brothers and I are on track to generate a quarter of a million profit in our first year of financial management."

His teeth flashed brilliantly white as he laughed and laughed. "Isn't that just a quaint little family business. Are you getting your Ma and Pa in on it too? Maybe they can help print paperwork or make meals while you and your brothers are so busy making all that money. I'm sure you'll enjoy the small closet you can work out of with all those hard-earned profits. Wow. Quarter of a million, huh?"

Jesus, this man was relentless. I bit my tongue, fighting back the choice words that swirled to the surface. I had to be *pleasant* Axel, *let-me-marry-your-daughter* Axel. Not *fuck-your-condescension-with-my-fist* Axel.

"I understand Cora's comfort and her safety are of the utmost importance to you, as her father," I went on, each word scraping past my lips. Other words wanted to replace them so badly, but I would not let them out. Not right now. Not until I could scream every last obscenity into my leather jacket in a corner of a subway station like a regular New Yorker. "I am prepared to prove to you how committed

I am to giving her the life she deserves. Sir—Allan—I love your daughter more than anything else in this world. I would do anything for her. And I mean that."

His lips curled away from his teeth in a sardonic grin. "Anything, huh?"

"Anything."

"Then fuck off."

I gritted my teeth, the hot swirl of anger dancing dangerously close to the tip of my tongue. *Do not call him a pretentious asshole. Do not call him a disgusting fucktard. Do not call him a pompous narcissist who makes Donald Trump look humble.*

"I said I'd do anything to prove that I am committed to giving her the life she deserves," I reminded him as neutrally as my internal rage would allow. "If I fuck off, sir, Allan, *Mr. Margulis,* then I can't give her the life she deserves."

"Ah, so you want to play word games. Fine. Let's play. You want my blessing for a marriage that is doomed to fail? Then let's start from scratch. If you want to even consider the laughable notion of becoming a part of *my* family, then you need to drop the smartass attitude. Ditch your plans. Even though I know that meager 250K sounds like a gold mine, I assure you, it's not. You commit 100% to Margulis Realty and *then* we can see about having a conversation about this under your real name."

I couldn't tell if this was a joke or an action plan. I ground my teeth in thought. "Okay."

"Start at the bottom, and then maybe in a couple years we can reconvene."

Heat prickled across my shoulders. What he was saying did not—*could not*—fit into my vision for the future. But maybe I needed to buck up and accept it.

"I'm willing," was all I could say even though there was so much unsaid writhing inside me.

"Great. You can find an application at the front desk on your way out." Allan sank back into his seat.

I blinked a few times. "You mean I have to apply for a job here?"

His laughter rang out sharp and unapologetic. He absolutely fucking loved this, and I hated him for it. But if I wanted Cora, I had to take the beating.

"I think there's an opening right now, so you have a good shot of being hired." He sniffed, immersing himself in his paperwork once more. "If nothing else, we're always looking for janitors. Ten dollars an hour, and it will get you in the door." He glanced up at me. "After all, you'll do anything, won't you?"

This time, it was my turn to laugh. "You'd rather I walk away from 250 thousand dollars in profit to take your below poverty-level job?"

"I need you to show your commitment to the Margulis family." He was unfazed. What an absolute, unrepentant bastard.

"By scrubbing your toilets."

Allan blinked dramatically, as if he profoundly did not understand my issue. "Is it the type of work that's stopping you? I figured you'd feel more at home at that level. Isn't that how your father made his thousands?"

His thousands. I could have drowned in the sea of condescension he'd filled the room with. My adoptive father wasn't a janitor. But my biological father had been. How Allan knew that was anybody's guess. I doubted Cora had given him the rundown of my sorry family history. Which meant Allan had been doing his homework, even while actively loathing me.

He'd prodded deeper than I'd expected.

"Listen," I began, expelling a defeated burst of air. But nothing followed it. I had nothing left to offer him that wouldn't ruin what miniscule chance I still had left. He'd beaten me down, and I'd held back the insults.

Allan checked his watch. "Your time's up, boy. It was real nice talking to you." In an exaggerated southern accent, he added, "Y'all come back now, hear?"

"Fuck you," I said. The glare this prompted served as the final push over the edge of my restraint. "You want to talk about lack of respect. Every last fucking thing you've said to me in here was the definition of disrespectful."

"Look around, you naïve child. You're in my building. Enjoying my view. Breathing *my* air." He wasn't wrong, since buying air rights in the city was common practice. He hefted with a scoff. "I don't owe you shit. Now take a good look around, because this is the last time you'll ever see the inside of my world."

Anger slashed at my chest. I had to leave. *Now.* Allan thought he'd won, but this battle wasn't fucking over. I tore myself out of his office, hurt and bewilderment crowding the edges of my vision. I could barely see where I was going, yet somehow I made it into the elevator. I paced the small box as it plummeted downward, tugging at my hair as I struggled to take deep, calming breaths.

Nothing would have given me more pleasure than to smash his face in, but I'd have to settle for imagined acts of vandalism.

In my head, I was pissing all over his office and swinging a bat against the glass flames sculpture in the lobby as I stormed out of the elevator. I was so angry I almost forgot my jacket, so I had to stomp back across the gleaming floor to snag it. All eyes fell on me—maybe I was seething too hard—but I couldn't give a fuck.

The only thing keeping me from actually pissing in the lobby was the fact that I still planned on marrying Cora. Trace's voice of reason echoed in my head as I tugged my coat on and headed for the revolving glass doors of the north entrance. *"If you piss in his lobby, you know he'll pay off all the town clerks in the tri-state area to make sure your marriage license doesn't go through."* Imaginary Trace was probably right.

I didn't need to give him more ammunition against me, because Cora and I were getting married.

No matter what Asshole Margulis thought.

CHAPTER SIX

CORA

"Cora, can you come to the table now?" My mother's voice at my ear dragged me out of my thoughts. I'd been glued to my phone all evening. Something was up with Axel, but he wasn't saying what. It had been twelve hours since I'd seen him, but my skin already itched from wanting more of him. It was always like this when we could finally see each other. The longing overruled everything else. He awakened something so primal and so intense within me that I could barely function after our meetups.

"I'm waiting on my lemons," I said weakly, gesturing toward the bartender at the other end of the bar. We were at Hallow, an upscale restaurant located in a converted cathedral. Everything glinted gold and heavenly, the remnants of the saintly influence, no doubt.

"Have them bring it to you at the table." My mother was using her stage voice, which was soft and hid the annoyance lurking underfoot. Only I could hear how agitated she truly was with me.

"I know, but—" I swallowed hard. I did not want to see any of the people who had gathered at our table. "He's cutting it fresh. Besides, you know they always forget to bring enough lemon."

She lowered her head and sent me a direct glare. "I'll see you at the table."

My mother wound through the crowd, leaving me feeling like a little girl in trouble. My parents had a specific way of making everyone yield to their desires. Their manipulations were often subtle and prolonged, and after enough time, became the same as a python squeeze. In the end, you'd agree to what you'd never considered possible.

I'd walked into this expecting the squeeze. I knew what awaited me at that table. And being aware was half the battle. I needed it to be.

When the bartender returned with my small plate of perfect lemon wedges, I grinned. Small pleasures kept me going. I snapped a picture and sent it to Axel: *My basic bitch lemons are ready.*

I tucked my phone into my Hermes leather handbag and slid the bartender a ten-dollar bill before winding through the packed restaurant with my prize. I'd walked into this knowing it was a business meeting, which was why I'd worn a simple black high-necked dress and matching heels. My pink goat skin handbag was the only acceptable flair for a meeting like this. But even though this was overtly a business reunion, I knew there was so much *more* on the line than just business—which was why I was prepared to lollygag, divert, and annoy.

"Cora! There you are!" My mother's bright voice frayed at the edges as she called out to me over the din. I'd "gotten lost" on my way to the table, and her waving hand shot into the air to guide me.

"Oh, boy." I offered a big but fake smile as I approached the round table, set for six. *The Margulis/Rossberg party.* "Almost wandered right out onto the street." Which was what I wished had happened.

"Cora! It's so good to see you again." Eli's parents stood to greet me, his mother coming toward me with a warm smile and outstretched arms. From day one she'd treated me as a surrogate daughter. We'd only met a handful of times, and to be fair, I did like the woman. She'd always been sweet with me. But my mother could be sweet with me, too, and that didn't mean the python squeeze wasn't waiting at the end.

"You look bright eyed and bushy tailed, as usual," Eli's father told me as he shook my hand briefly. Eli himself waited behind his parents, a small smile on his lips. His moss-green gaze settled on me, blond tresses arranged in a perfect finger wave. He was twenty-three like me, but his arrogance added a few extra years, made him look older.

"Eli, good to see you," I said curtly, offering my cheek for the requisite peck. He pressed his hand against my back—which he normally did *not* do—and brought me in closer to him.

"I'm so happy you agreed to this meeting," he murmured into my ear. "You're hard to catch, you know that?"

"Excuse me?" I pulled back.

He watched me as if he knew a secret. Like maybe my father had promised him something. "Let's just say it's good to know that money is what makes you purr."

I felt like that comment deserved a slap on the cheek, though I wasn't entirely sure why. What had been said behind closed doors? My mother urged me to sit down in the chair beside her, leaving the last empty seat for my father, who had been held up at the office. I swallowed my frustration at Eli's comment and sat down—of course right at Eli's side.

"So, Cora, tell us—how have classes been?" Eli's mother gushed.

"Oh, June, give her a moment to order a drink at least," her husband chided with an apologetic look my way. "What are you drinking, Cora? Whiskey, neat? Or maybe a sauvignon blanc."

I laughed politely. "Water is fine. A chardonnay wouldn't hurt."

While Eli's father worked on flagging down a server, my mother folded her hands on the tabletop. "Allan should be here shortly. It's not like him to be so tardy."

"Maybe a meeting ran over," Eli suggested.

"I'm sure he has a very good reason," June said.

The knot in my gut cinched tighter. I didn't know why my father was late, but it was weird. Axel wasn't replying to me, which was also weird. All of that on top of staring at the weirdness around me made me feel like I could drown.

"We don't want him to miss a second of our discussion," Jeffrey said, grinning as a server approached. He crossed his arms and sent a too-wide smile up to the young lady. "Please, the most expensive chardonnay in the building. A bottle."

"I certainly don't need a bottle," I said.

"It's for celebrating afterward," Jeffrey explained. "With Eli."

"Once us old people leave," June added with a breezy laugh.

There would be no celebrating with Eli—that much was certain. A business deal didn't need to infringe on my after hours. Besides, I would find any excuse necessary to spend the night at Axel's.

"I think this dinner should be celebration enough," I said. "Look at where we are! We're practically exalting right now."

Eli leaned back in his seat, propping his hand on the back of my chair. I leaned closer to the table, reaching for my water glass so I could plunk the appropriate number of lemons into it—three—and get the hell away from his smarmy reach.

There wasn't anything inherently wrong with Eli. He was just your average wealthy jerk. Famous parents, wealth beyond imagination, a lucky mixture of gene pools. I couldn't deny that Eli was attractive. Square jaw, a disarming smile that showcased perfect white teeth. His stare had jolted me a time or two in our private high school. But the tall, blond, and mossy mix was no match for Axel's dirty blond Kentucky charm. He could fix a tractor *and* get me off. Most men couldn't do either.

Our parents occasionally spotted someone they knew in the restaurant, pausing to wave or send a quick smile to a colleague. It was like this everywhere we went. The elite circle of the city was small. We all knew each other. Knew who belonged, who didn't.

That was what made Axel's business idea so fragile. Men like Eli and his father—my father, too—would never allow him into their circle. His pool of potential big-ticket clients was smaller than he'd planned on. Very few men held unimaginable power. Which was why Axel's plan needed to be rock-solid to break into the industry like he and his brothers were planning.

"Sorry, sorry, everyone." The rough voice of my father broke through our dull chitchat. I straightened, offering a generic smile as my father made his rounds greeting everyone. He eased into the empty seat beside my mother. "I hope you all weren't waiting too long."

"Don't even worry about it, Allan," Jeffrey said. "Your beautiful wife ordered your favorite drink while we were waiting, and we've gotten caught up on Cora's courses for this semester. All's well."

My father nodded, looking at the tumbler of high-end whiskey—his preferred drink—as though he didn't recognize it.

"How was work today?" my mom began, in lieu of saying *What the fuck is wrong with you?*

My father cleared his throat, finally reaching for the tumbler and giving it a swirl. He still hadn't looked at me. "A busy day, as usual. Had a surprise meeting at the end that ran over, though."

"Oh? New plans for hotel somewhere?" A conspiratorial smirk stretched at Jeffrey's lips. "Let me guess. Dubai."

My father laughed, but it was hollow. "No. Just another wishful idiot who thinks he can run things his own way."

Jeffrey groaned. "God, they never stop, do they?"

"This one was worse than most." My father's jaw worked back and forth, and finally he looked at me, something dark twisting at his face. "Comes with the territory I guess."

"I say, fire them the second they show signs of insubordination." Jeffrey emphasized his point by punching the air. "We don't need them. And apparently they don't need us."

"But what if they don't work for you?"

"Then just have them ruined," Eli said with a laugh.

My father's smile fell quickly as he took a healthy gulp of his drink. When the glass hit the table, he rolled his neck from side to side. "I'm ready for this meeting to start. And to get some damn food in my stomach."

"I ordered an appetizer or two already," my mother purred.

"Great. Let's cut to the chase. Jeffrey?" My father's lips curled up in what looked like a genuine smile. Shocking.

Jeffrey retuned the smile, then looked over at me. "Cora, you brilliant next-gen businesswoman, you. I want you on my team."

A shocked laugh fluttered out of me. "Why, Jeffrey, that's so sweet of you—"

"Your coursework at Stanford puts you in a unique position to work in tandem with our company. But what I'm seeing on the horizon is bigger than just your regular collaboration. I want Margulis Realty to come along for the ride. Into *space*, of course, but also into the boardroom."

I nodded slowly, fragments from my initial phone conversation with my father floating back into my head. "Of course."

"Imagine your father's hotels on the moon. The first ever Margulis office building erected on Mars. When space tourism hits—which it will, and *soon*—we need a social innovator on our side to help navigate the new terrain."

It all sounded so wild, almost made up. But the kernel of opportunity there excited me. How could it not? "That sounds...incredible."

"So you agree a merger would be brilliant." Jeffrey's smile was ear to ear as his gaze shifted from Eli to June. "Well, this makes my job a lot easier."

"I can't imagine a more ingenious next step than linking Margulis Realty with Rossberg Aerospace. I wish it had been my idea," my father grumbled.

"Let's say it was both of our ideas," Jeffrey offered. "After all, our inspiration was right in front of us." His eyes crinkled at the edges as he looked between Eli and me. "Though I guess I shouldn't get ahead of myself. Have you decided to join the family company once you finish your MBA?"

I schooled my face not to betray any of the emotions this issue usually brought up: annoyance, indecision, utter disinterest. "Those negotiations are still underway."

Jeffrey's eyes widened, and he sent an impressed look toward my father. "You've taught her well."

"Perhaps too well," my father said, crossing his arms.

"How could she not go into the family business?" Eli asked coolly, and it reeked of being for my father's benefit. After all, he was sitting right next to me. If Axel were here, I knew what he'd call him: a pompous turdmuffin.

"Maybe you could ask her," I said a bit quieter, strictly for Eli's benefit.

"Well, I suppose that does put a damper on the conversation," Jeffrey said, looking disappointed in the way an actor on Broadway might—overdone a bit, so the audience in the last row can still feel it. "We're interested in working with the next generation of Margulis Realty. Though I'm sure the alternatives you're entertaining are...worthy."

My father coughed. My mother reached for her wine.

"Point is, I'm seeing an incredible team right here." Jeffrey made a square between him, my father, Eli and me. "Yes, our flagship businesses have found incredible success." He clapped my father on his shoulder, but pinned me with a deep look. "But we're thinking about the future here. We want to be at the front of this race to develop space, not coming in second or third. And I think it's something my grandchildren will actively be participating in as well."

"Your grandchildren?" I echoed as both June and my mother erupted into laughter.

"I thought we were the ones supposed to be putting on the pressure?" My mother asked wryly.

"As long as there's pressure, I'm not sure it matters who applies it," Jeffrey responded.

"Oh, Jeffrey." June feigned annoyance, but secret pleasure rolled off her. The way her gaze darted between Eli and me served as a billboard for her thoughts: *Just get married already and give me grandbabies!*

I had no intention of marrying Eli. Ever. He was handsome, but that's where my admiration began and ended.

The only man I was interested in procreating with wasn't welcome at this table. But I couldn't think about that tangle right now. Every man here wanted something from me, and I didn't want to give any of them even half of what they hoped for.

"I hope it doesn't bother any of you that I'm not planning on having children," I said once their laughter subsided. It wasn't strictly true, but they didn't need to know that.

"You'll change your mind," June assured me. "I said the same at your age."

"Cora," my mother started, her tone dripping with *don't start*.

"Aren't we getting ahead of ourselves?" Eli broke in, squeezing my shoulder. His touch made me tingle, but not for a good reason. "After all, it's way too early to talk about that. There are businesses to run."

"At least we agree on that," I told him.

"Fine. We'll table the grandchildren for a later meeting," Jeffrey conceded. "But we can't let the future of this Margulis-Rossberg merger get away from us. That's why we need to act now. Look at all this talent around us. All this opportunity. We'd be negligent to let it slip away."

Dinner churned forward, punctuated with Asian pear salads, lamb shank, expensive wine, and unending chatter about business. The attention turned from my childbearing and business merger potential, thankfully, but Eli buzzed with interest at my side and it was all I could do not to tell him to fuck off. That was Axel's influence, no doubt—he had a way with words, but he did not hesitate to scrap the finesse and resort to a good old *fuck off* when necessary.

When the chardonnay and lamb shanks were tucked away inside me, I saw my chance to snag my handbag and head for the bathroom. Curiosity clawed at me, wondering if Axel had replied. I excused myself, grabbed my purse, and bolted for the ladies room.

Inside the mauve and taupe tiled paradise, where fragrance oils gave the mundane a touch of the elegant, I leaned against the wall and scrolled through my phone.

AXEL: Babe, where are you?

AXEL: I need you. I need to see you. Like, NOW.

CORA: What's wrong? Just saw these texts. I'm at dinner with my parents.

Three dots appeared on the screen as Axel typed. I wriggled with anticipation, gnawing on my upper lip.

AXEL: What's on the agenda for after? I've got a surprise cooking.

CORA: Just tell me where to go and I'm there. I'll figure it out.

After I had tucked my phone away and tinkled, I stared at my reflection in the oval mirror. I'd opted for a nude lip gloss to complement my sharp business dress. My dark brown hair was gathered to one side, obscuring the hint of a bruise Axel had left on my neck last night. I'd covered it well with concealer, but one could never be too cautious in these situations.

I smirked at my reflection as I dried my hands. Shivers raced through me, remembering how Axel had bitten his way up my spine, across the underside of my breasts, and to the fleshy parts of my neck. He'd left no part of me untouched last night. I was still trapped in the fantasy of last night as I left the bathroom, hardly aware of my surroundings until I crashed into someone.

Eli, to be exact.

"Hey, sorry," he said, gripping me by the sides of my arms. "I didn't mean for you to run into me, though I can't say I mind."

"Maybe if you didn't lurk outside of the women's restroom, stuff like that wouldn't happen," I said, stepping away from him. He stepped with me, blocking the exit to the dining room.

"Can you blame me? You're so hard to get, Cora. You love to play that game, don't you?"

"I'm not playing a game, Eli," I told him, my irritation ballooning to new heights. "I went to the bathroom, and now you're in my way."

"Can't you just give me a chance?" he asked. Something in his tone broke through the irritation. He was being sincere, or as close to sincere as was possible for him. I'd known him since elementary school, but only from a distance. I didn't know the terrains of his heart or what he acted like in his down time. This fleeting glimpse of vulnerability caught me off guard.

"A chance for what?" I asked. "You know perfectly well that I have a boyfriend."

His eyes sharpened. "Has he proposed to you?"

"No." I swallowed. "Not yet. Why?"

"Then he's not going to. Besides, there's nothing that says we can't talk about our *own* future," Eli pressed on. "That kid can't handle a woman like you. I can. Promise me you'll give me a chance."

I rolled my eyes. "You know nothing about my boyfriend and what he plans to do. But sure. In the alternate universe where I'm somehow dissatisfied with the love of my life, yeah, I'd give you a chance." I held up my palm as I edged past him, creating a barrier between his intentions and my body.

I didn't make it five steps before Eli called out to me.

"You know I could have him ruined, right?"

I turned to look at him. "Are you really that hard up, Eli? You don't need to do that. In fact, you don't need me at all. Just go find a girlfriend, literally anyone else."

His jaw flexed, a smile tugging at his lips. "You know it just turns me on when you play hard to get."

I expelled a frustrated sigh and turned on my heel. That was the last thing I cared about. "See you at the table."

But Eli's words followed me closely.

I could have him ruined.

Eli wasn't exaggerating.

And no matter how much I wanted to pretend his interest didn't matter to me, I still needed to figure out just how serious he was.

CHAPTER SEVEN

AXEL

CORA: Where are you?

AXEL: I'm waiting outside for you babe. I'll come get you.

I pocketed my phone, my heart racing so fast I felt like I might tip over face-first into the sidewalk. This was the best I could come up with—an impromptu date night on the heels of the biggest, loudest no I'd ever received in my life. I still hadn't properly recovered from that abysmal meeting with Allan, but I didn't have time to process.

I needed to make Cora my fiancée. Immediately.

I hoped my swagger hid the wobble in my knees as I paced outside the building on Park Avenue. I'd sent her the address with no context, with barely enough cash on me to cover what would probably end up being the most expensive drinks in the city. But this lounge was worth it, a place I'd stumbled upon entirely by accident thanks to the friend of a business school classmate not too long ago. And whatever money I didn't spend on drinks I was giving to the server upstairs as a payment to capture this proposal in pictures and video.

Now all she had to do was say yes and the rest of our lives could begin.

The Meridian Lounge was the perfect mixture of upscale fancy and sultry moodiness. It seemed like the same blend as what

Cora and I had to look forward to, as well. Trendy. Put together. Arousingly glamorous yet still approachable. Right smack dab in the middle of Manhattan.

I spotted her stepping out of the rideshare at the corner. Her toned legs glistened, which meant she'd used the shimmer lotion for this evening. Jesus, I loved it when she used the shimmer lotion. All my anxiety dissolved as she swung her smoky eyes my way. No other woman in the world could be more gorgeous, more perfect, than my Cora. My throat squeezed with emotion as she walked toward me, a velvety black coat pulled tight around her, that too-expensive-to-be-real pink goatskin bag dangling from the crook of her elbow.

"You just gonna stare at me all day?" she teased.

I pulled her into my arms, relief flooding me. She was my woman. Now and forever. I wasn't sure how I'd gotten lucky enough to find her, but life had brought her to me. Fuck, I was going to start crying before I even got near to proposing.

"Axel, are you okay?" she pulled back to look at me. I cleared my throat, wondering if she could see the sheen of tears in my eyes.

"Yeah. Totally fine, babe." I pressed a soft kiss to her lips, cupping her heart-shaped face in my hands. "I can't wait to show you this place."

I took her hand, double-checking discreetly with my other hand that the ring box was still in my pocket. I led her into the cavernous lobby of the building, following gold-flecked signs reading *Meridian* on the pillars between the door and the elevator. Another couple joined us on the ride up, but we barely noticed them. All I could see was Cora. I held her gathered against me all the way to the thirteenth floor. The doors slid open, revealing abstract zebra print rugs and gauzy amber lighting. The lounge was packed with all levels of cool—hipsters and trendy businesspeople alike, leaning together on low wooden benches and minimalist wire-framed wing chairs.

Cora let out a low hum of approval as I led her through the attractive fray. "Now this is a lovely spot."

"I knew you'd love it." I pressed a kiss to her cheek and opened the door for the terrace. It was a chilly evening, but the fire of our love and commitment would keep us warm. Besides, celebratory drinks lay on the other side of this proposal. We'd be toasty in no time.

"Should we get drinks?" Cora asked.

"In a minute." The uninterrupted vista of the downtown skyline commanded our attention. Even after living here for five years, it still took my breath away. I wasn't sure I'd ever get used to being a resident of New York, after being stuck in the hills of Kentucky for most of my life. Some days I could see Manhattan through the veneer of my childhood aspirations, where even the traffic jams exhilarated me.

"Oh, Axel." Her voice came out a reverent whisper as we tucked ourselves into a plant-lined corner overlooking the city. Tall space heaters dotted the terrace, which made the cold night bearable. "This is beautiful."

Not quite as stunning as the view from her father's office, though I didn't want to bring up how I knew that. The murmur of other patrons on the terrace faded away as my anxiety returned. It was now or never. My mouth went dry. I touched the outline of the small ring box in my pocket.

"It doesn't compare to how beautiful you are," I said and nudged her.

She smirked, catching on to my too-corny-to-be-real vibe. "Are you trying to pick me up with that line?"

"Only if I wanted you to head straight for the door." I looked back toward the bar, searching for the server who'd I'd slipped a hundo in advance. I caught his eye and jerked my head. He shot me a thumbs up and headed our way. Looking back at Cora, I said, "I know better than to compare you to a bustling metropolis."

"I guess for some people, city-to-human comparisons do the job," she mused, gaze sweeping out over the glowing night horizon.

"Some people are turned on by bridges. Sometimes inanimate objects are hot, if you're into that." I swallowed hard, shouting at myself to get the show on the road. I shoved my hand into my pocket. *Just fucking do it. Stop talking about this weirdo shit.*

She threw her head back and laughed. "Like how I'm turned on by your leather jacket?"

I slung my arm over her shoulders, bringing her in close. "You just like what's underneath the leather jacket."

She turned toward me, looking up into my eyes. I had her full attention, and I was sweating bullets. *Now. The time is now.* I grabbed her arms. "Cora."

Her smile dropped a little. "Axel."

I drew a shaky breath. Her father was going to be so fucking pissed. But I had to plunge ahead, consequences be damned. We were meant for each other, and we both knew it. "You know why I brought you here tonight?"

"Because we like getting drinks in pretty places?"

"Yes, that." I laughed, kissing her forehead. "But I also have a really important question for you."

Her eyes went round. "Oh my god. Are you serious?" She clamped her hands over her mouth and a squeal leaked out.

"Cora—don't—"

"Axel, oh my god, oh my god, are you going to ask me?" She fanned her face. Tears pooled in her eyes.

Over her shoulder, I spotted the server stealthily capturing the moment. All I could do was laugh. "I mean, yes, but you aren't supposed to call me out about it."

She wiped away a tear. "Oh my god, I'm sorry, I'm ruining it." She fanned her face again. "Shit. Oh my god, I'm ruining it."

"You aren't ruining it." I kissed her forehead again, so amused I could burst. "I was just going to ask you if you wanted to spend the night at my house."

Her eyes widened again but for a different reason. Laughter rolled out of me. This was it. Everything was perfect. I slowly sank to one knee and her mouth formed a big O.

"Oh my god, you *are* going to ask me," she whispered hoarsely.

I fished the ring box out of my pocket and clamped it in my hand. I'd had a million different monologues planned. But none of it mattered. I didn't need to get it perfect with her. Because what we did was perfect for us. "Cora Jean Margulis. I've wanted to make you my wife since the week after we met. I knew from the beginning that you were it for me. The woman I've waited my entire life to meet. And I'll spend the rest of our lives proving that I'm worthy of being at your side."

She sobbed softly, a hand clamped against her mouth.

"Cora Jean," I said, popping open the ring box. "My cowgirl. My sweet cheeks. Will you marry me?"

She blinked out some tears and collapsed on top of me, arms cinching around my neck. She cried into my neck, repeating "Yes" over and over again. The ring didn't matter. It was about the love between us. It was a small detail, but it just reaffirmed what I knew to be true.

"I love you so much, babe." Tears pooled in my eyes and spilled over. From across the terrace, the server gave me a thumbs up and I returned it. Applause broke out around us, and Cora's tears turned into laughter.

"I forgot there were other people here," she whispered.

"They love that you just agreed to marry me."

Her lips found mine, two grins meeting. Our salt-stained kisses grew deeper and more passionate. I pumped the brakes when I started getting hard right there on the terrace with an audience.

"Don't you want to see the ring, babe?" I murmured into her ear. She laughed again, and we both stood. She peered inside the ring box and clamped a hand over her mouth.

"It's so gorgeous, Axel. It's exactly what I've always dreamt of. How are you so perfect?" She was blubbering now as I slid the ring onto her finger. Once it was in place, she flung her arms around me again. "How did you manage—"

"Shhh. We don't need to talk about that right now." I stroked her hair, and we started swaying back and forth. As if on cue, a romantic jazzy electronic song drifted from the bar. Yet another sign that this was right. Everything would be fine. It didn't matter what Allan said or thought. He couldn't intrude on the love we had for each other.

Cora squeezed me so tight around my waist that I coughed. She looked up at me, eyes shining. "I'll be Mrs. Fairchild."

"God, that sounds sexy."

"I'll change my passport so it shows my new name."

"You trying to write your vows right now? Because that's what it sounds like."

The server came over to me, and I thanked him, slipping him another hundred dollar bill. Cheaper than a photographer at least, and I offered him a discount on financial management services if he ever needed them. As my phone began vibrating with the photos he sent my way, I brought Cora's knuckles to my lips.

"Let's celebrate with a drink. I'm buying. You stay here and enjoy the view, Future Mrs. Fairchild." I pressed a kiss to her forehead and headed across the terrace, looking back every few seconds to lock eyes with her and grin like an idiot. Inside the bar, the volume had risen—more people, more chatter, more frenetic notes of electronic jazz music. I headed toward the bartender with a perma-grin, ordering two of Cora's favorite: gin and tonic.

When the bartender told me the total, I slid him my debit card. He swiped it and grimaced. "It said declined. Do you have another form of payment?"

Panic streaked through me. I'd just given most of my cash to the server and these drinks were pushing fifty dollars. "Yeah. Hang on." I fumbled for my wallet, pulling out a credit card I kept on hand. Except it was damn near maxed out. I sent up a thousand prayers while the bartender swiped it. *Please don't do this to me today. Not when we're so happy.* He stared at the screen of his console blankly, and then handed back the card as a receipt printed. I let out a low breath of relief.

I added a tip, though I wasn't sure if the extra amount would go through, and signed with a flourish. One of my brothers had to have used our shared debit card accidentally, but I wasn't going to investigate now. I headed back onto the terrace with our drinks, finding Cora frowning in the corner next to the space heater, staring down at her phone.

"Cheers, babe."

She looked up at me, that pretty smile returning. We clinked glasses as I eased into the seat next to her. After a sip, she hummed. "That hits the spot."

"I figured it would. And I'll hit your other spot later."

She giggled, her hand coming to my chest. "There's the pick-up line that works on me." She nuzzled my neck. "I love you so much, Axel."

"I love you more."

"So when should we have the wedding?" She cozied up to me even further, and I lifted her legs so they rested on my lap.

Dragging my hand back and forth across the shimmery smoothness there, I said, "I want whatever date you want."

"This wedding planning is off to a great start. Giving me all the control." She laughed evilly and then sipped her drink again. "I've always wanted one of those redundant dates. Like 2-22. Or 4-4."

"We can get it etched into a cutting board, hang it in the kitchen."

"Where should our first house be?"

"Wherever you want, honey." I grinned again, capturing a sweet kiss. God, it felt good to say that. But my anxiety tugged at me. I had a maxed-out credit card to offer her as we started our lives together. *You're fucking this up already.* I took another hard pull at my drink, needing the heat that would calm my monkey brain. *What if your business doesn't launch like you think?* Another hard pull. *Maybe Allan was right.*

"Jeez, drink it all in one gulp," she teased me.

"These expensive drinks taste better," I croaked, swirling what little was left in my glass. "Anyway, I was thinking we could have a condo in the city. Then probably a country house in Kentucky, by my parents. Then an LA pad, for whenever we start conquering the West Coast."

She giggled, nuzzling against me. "Can I decorate all the houses?"

"Of course, babe." *Except when will you be able to afford all these houses? When you're both 70?* "Whatever Mrs. Fairchild wants, Mrs. Fairchild gets."

She bit her bottom lip, pinning me with the sexiest look I've ever seen. "I'm not kidding Axel, if you say that one more time I might come right now."

Oof. Like there was any challenge I wanted to accept more than this one. I wet my bottom lip and surveyed the terrace. There weren't too many people out here, due to the cold, but with how close we were to the space heater and how happy we were from the fresh engagement, we could have been out here naked. I slipped my leather coat off and covered her legs. My hand found the heat underneath her dress. She lowered her chin, a sexy smile playing at her lips.

"What was that, Mrs. Fairchild?"

Her nostrils flared as my fingers found the soaked crotch of her panties. So the proposal had turned her on. Our foreheads came together as I pushed my fingertips to meet the swollen heat of her. She was juicy velvet, crushed and electric. With one finger inside of her I snagged a deep, sloppy tongue kiss. Her thighs went rigid beneath my leather coat.

"You make this too easy," I whispered hotly into her ear, "when you're turned on like this. Dripping wet. And all because you're about to be my wife."

"It's your fault," she said breathily. I circled my fingers around the hard nub of her clit, and she jolted in my arms. "You're the only man who makes marriage look like a good idea."

I coaxed another passionate kiss from her while I eased a second finger into her, then a third. She loved being filled with me—wherever and however possible. And the night of our engagement called for something to remember.

I swiped my thumb back and forth over the needy nub while I pumped my fingers into her forcefully. She whimpered softly, tightening her grip around my neck.

"I'm ready to fingerfuck you in public for the rest of our lives."

A lazy smile drifted onto her face, and she arched against me slightly just as a server flitted up to our table.

"Anything else you two need right now?"

I plunged my fingers into the velvety heat of her pussy and flashed a big smile to the server. "I think we're fine. Right, Cora?"

Cora cleared her throat and then let out a squeak, her thighs rigid beneath the coat. She was so close to coming. I pinched her clit between my thumb and forefinger, her juices dripping down my hand. The server drifted away, none the wiser, and I captured Cora's lips in a kiss.

"Come for me, Mrs. Fairchild."

Her thighs went rock hard around my hand. The whimper was the only external sign that she'd crossed the ledge, but beneath my leather jacket I could feel the way her pussy pulsed around my fingers, drawing them deeper into her. Only I could sense how her breaths had turned feathery and hurried.

My entire body itched with the need to plunge my cock into her, to give her every inch of my passion. But not here. We'd never fool a server if I was allowed to fuck her properly.

I nibbled on her ear lobe as her orgasm subsided, sweeping lazy circles around her throbbing clit.

"That was just the pre-party," I whispered into her ear. "Proper celebration to come."

"I wish I didn't have to fly back Sunday morning."

"I'll come out soon," I told her, the declined message from my debit card flashing behind my lids. "I'll make it work." Even though I had no idea how to make it work. Our future depended on it.

She shifted against me, opening her mouth to say something. But in lieu of words, she gasped. I withdrew my hand from beneath her dress on instinct. Her feet shot to the floor, gaze stuck at the entrance to the bar.

"Jesus, it's Vince." She clutched at the leather jacket over her lap, as though my fingers were still buried knuckle deep. Her neck flushed, and she reached for her drink. "Why the fuck is he here," she muttered above the rim of her glass.

Her father's driver was part chauffer, part bodyguard. The man was one of those mafia-for-hire types, your run-of-the-mill, take-no-shit Brooklyn dudes who would not hesitate to break your wrist and then threaten to sue for the inconvenience of having to break your wrist.

He was the sort of guy I wanted on my side...and the sort of guy I dreaded having to deal with when he was on Allan's side.

"We can leave," I offered. "The tab is closed."

"Like we can escape now." Her throat bobbed, and she swore under her breath. "He just saw us."

Vince frowned his way over to us. We were in trouble, though I didn't know why. Unless Allan could *sense* that I'd asked his daughter to marry me.

"What are you doing here?" Cora hissed when Vince was within hearing range.

"Get your stuff. Car's downstairs." He snapped his fingers and jerked his thumb in the direction of the door. "Pronto, little lady."

"I'm busy," Cora said through clenched teeth.

"Don't matta. There's an emergency. Let's go." Vince crossed his wrists and waited, leaving no room for debate.

"I'll take her," I said.

Vince hefted with a laugh. "That's funny. You ready, Cora?"

"My father is capable of speaking to me himself." She straightened her back. "I don't understand what could be so important."

"He'll explain when you get to the hospital."

Cora's eyes widened, and she turned to me. In a low voice, she said, "I should go, right?"

I worked my jaw back and forth. The whole thing was a little fucked up, but she didn't want to be on the wrong side of an emergency. Despite what I felt about the man, he was her father.

"Yeah. We'll meet up after, okay?"

She nodded and reached for her purse, pressing a quick kiss to my lips. Her toned body stretched out as she stood, the shimmer of her calves snagging my attention once more. I reached for her as she walked away, my fingertips brushing the black hem of her dress.

Even though she had to leave, there was still reason to celebrate.

The engagement ring glittered on her left hand as she walked toward the door.

Leaving or not, Cora was mine.

CHAPTER EIGHT

CORA

Vince didn't give up any information the entire ride. He was famous for being a brick when my father ordered him to be, which chafed worse and worse until we arrived at my parents' building. Vince accompanied me into the back elevator, stoic and thick-necked like always. Sometimes, on our good days, he was like a surrogate father to me. But most of the time, he was my actual father's irritating hired grunt.

"You said we were going to the hospital," I reminded Vince as he swiped the keycard before punching the button for the penthouse.

"Did I?" A smirk materialized on his face.

"I'm going to be so pissed if there's no medical emergency." I glared at the wall of the elevator as we soared upward toward the thirty-third floor. My body already knew the truth. There was no medical emergency. And now I had to prepare myself for...something. The not knowing was stressful, but I was used to it. My entire life had been wrought with the tension of waiting for the next round of bad news.

I'd thought after Chris's death that there could be no more bad news. After all, it couldn't get worse than losing my brother to suicide, right? But I'd been naïve then. All it meant was that the bad news got worse.

The elevator doors slid open, revealing the pristine back foyer of my parents' penthouse. The lights were dimmed, and there was no noise save the hum of the elevator. Vince gestured for me to step off.

I'd been expecting a welcoming party, so this lack of immediate news unnerved me even more. Light spilled from the hallway leading to the kitchen, and I headed that way. From deeper inside the house, there was a muffled sob. My stomach twisted into a knot.

"Bernadette, we're going to." My father's stern voice wafted down the hallway as I went deeper into the house. "It's time. I'm not going to say it again."

"Hello?" I slowed, gripping the strap of my purse. The weight of my new engagement ring reminded me of the big news I had. Now wasn't the best time. I slipped it off my finger and tucked it into my Hermes bag.

"Cora. Come in." My mother's voice sounded watery and thin. I rounded the corner into the kitchen and found them huddled together at the dinette, a stack of loose, curling, legal-pad yellow pages between them. The tight nut of my stomach dropped to the floor. Whatever news awaited me, it wasn't good.

"Sit down," my father instructed.

"Is everything okay?" I drifted toward an open chair at the table. My mother's ostentatiously large mosaic vase spilled with white roses. She always made sure the house was filled with fresh blooms. And somehow, gut-wrenching anxiety and the lingering smell of roses both conjured equally strong memories of home.

My father drew a deep breath, his gaze on my mother. "Bernadette."

My mother pressed two fingertips to her forehead and rolled her lips inward.

"You guys are freaking me out. Just tell me already. What is going on?"

"There's something you need to see," my mother finally said. "Before you go back to LA."

My gaze dropped to the papers between us. She rustled through some, and it was only then that I noticed the handwriting. The faint chicken scratch, the hurried swipe of the uppercase As, the flourish of Y that I'd always loved in secret. The handwriting that my father had called "too gay."

My bottomed-out stomach rooted and sprouted tiny anxiety flowers. My throat tightened. This was Chris's handwriting. At the top of one: "Dear family."

This was a letter from Chris.

"We found this," my mother began, but stopped short, her throat bobbing.

"You need to read it," my father said brusquely. He held my gaze, something grave and imploring there. The last time I'd seen him like this was shortly after Chris's funeral, when he issued the family mandate to never talk about my brother's suicide openly. With anyone. Under any circumstances. The formal NDA came later, which I was forcefully encouraged to sign. At age eighteen and in the throes of distress, I signed it without a second thought.

Which was why the world thought Christopher Margulis had died in a freak kitchen accident. What really happened was he put a gun to his head in his bedroom, right before I got home from tennis practice my senior year of high school.

"I thought he didn't leave a suicide note," I forced past dry lips.

"He didn't. The letter was found in his desk." My father seemed like he wanted to add more, but he clamped his mouth shut.

"You two were so incredibly close," my mother said, but this time she couldn't control the emotion. She was the only one in the family who had ever openly cried about my brother—once. As for me, I had cried myself to sleep for two whole years. Had it ever been that way for my mom? Or maybe worse?

I reached out for her hand to give it a small squeeze. She didn't let me into the sadness of her heart. Or even the joys. Nobody did in the Margulis family.

"I just think you'll be interested to see what's in here," she finished in a whisper. "Take it with you and read it. But please take care of it. I would like it returned."

"Of course." My fingers trembled as I reached out to take the pages she handed me. My father's nostrils flared, and he cleared his throat.

"You have a lot to think about. You'll leave for the airport at ten tomorrow morning."

"Good night, Cora." My mother pressed a small kiss to the top of my head, and my parents stood, leaving me in the soft white light of the dinette. Swimming in anxiety. Flush with the scent of roses. The true markers of home.

I walked to my bedroom on shaky legs. Chris had taken his own life six years ago, when he was in the thick of business school, headed for the greatness my father had always intended for him.

There was just one small problem. Chris didn't conform to *all* of my father's expectations. *I'm as gay as the day is long,* he'd always say with a sad smile and a horrible southern accent that he used just because he knew it would make me giggle. It didn't matter that Chris kept his inclinations private. It didn't matter that we had a gay uncle (who the family also rejected). It didn't matter that we lived in "this day and age."

My father had expectations. Those expectations bred rules. Those rules became tight as a vice.

And after so many years in a vice, he could no longer breathe.

Texts from Axel lit up my phone as I settled into my bedroom. Through the big bay windows, the Hudson River sparkled in front of the glowing horizon. I toed off my heels, simultaneously shooting back a reply.

CORA: I'm home. Everything's okay, I guess. My parents just had some heavy news.

AXEL: What news?

CORA: I'm still finding out. I'll let you know.

I nibbled on my upper lip, looking at the faded yellow legal pad sheets, trying to imagine Chris writing this. Had he been crying? Did he write them and save them in advance of his suicide, or had he scribbled them out in a manic fit right before pulling the trigger? What bothered me most was not knowing the details of his final moments. Not being able to ascertain his lucidity.

My mom hadn't been lying. Chris and I had been practically twins, three years removed. We palled around in everything—even from our earliest times, when Chris was too eager for my parents' liking to join me in tea parties with my dolls. What started as tea party besties blossomed into the Dynamic Duo. I was the only one who could talk him down on his darkest days. I was the only one who knew where he *really* went on Thursday nights when my parents thought he was at investment club (hint: gay spa). I was the only one who knew how sensitive the caverns of his heart truly were.

I was the only one who could have stopped him from pulling the trigger.

The tears had pooled in the lap of my black dress before I realized I was crying. I just needed to read this and be done with it. The sadness was exhausting. I'd been exhausted for so long.

I drew a shaky breath and plunged in.

Chris had written three whole pages. There was no date, but it read like a living will. Except he wasn't dispersing personal objects. He was dispersing his plans for the rest of us.

For my mother: *Plant me in a garden. Keep my memories in your blooms and just think of me with a smile. That's all I want.*

For my father: *Find happiness in the next head of Margulis Realty. I'm sorry that it couldn't be me, but we both know I would have just disappointed you.*

For me: *Give our father what I can't. You're made for this, Corky. How amazing of a CEO will you be? You won't just step up, you'll step in, and make history along the way.*

His words landed like bittersweet medicine on my tongue. I'd wanted more from him since the day we laid him to rest, but to see how he envisioned the future felt like a shove in the wrong direction.

I reread everything a second time, then a third. It didn't take a genius to figure out why my parents had shown me this now. But what really pestered me was wondering how long they'd been sitting on this letter. Sometimes their words were more of what they wanted the story to be. The most convenient truth for their agenda.

I'd have been suspicious of this letter if it weren't absolutely dripping with Chris's beautiful chicken scratch.

I set the pages aside with a heavy heart, dark dots of tears on my mauve comforter.

Chris wants you to do the job he couldn't.

It was one detail—the request of a person no longer here.

But Chris pulsated with life inside my heart every single day. His spirit zoomed through my mind, punctuated the particular successes and horrors of Fashion Week every year, asked me if I *really* wanted pickle on my deli meat sandwich like I'd ordered (the answer was always yes, Spirit Chris).

If I didn't do what he wanted, I'd fucking hear about it.

I couldn't think about it anymore though. This was too much; it was too heavy. My father wanted a decision, and this letter practically made it for me. Even on our bad days, I would have done anything Chris asked of me. And now this?

Salty tears found the crease of my lips. I drew a shuddery breath and lay the pages on the makeup-cluttered surface of my vanity. As I did, I caught a glimpse of the frightening state of my face. Dark rivulets of mascara down my cheeks. Smeared lipstick. Puffy, red eyes that still had tears after six years of weeping for my brother.

Because one thing was true—I was alive, and he wasn't.

I was the only person left who could accomplish the things he'd longed for.

I hadn't been there to stop him. I hadn't intervened. I'd been too preoccupied with my own life to stop the downward spiral.

Now I was the only one left to spiral at all.

CHAPTER NINE

CORA

I awoke the next morning in a fog, the kind of heaviness that slides in after endless hours of sobbing. Still in my dress and makeup from the night before, I stumbled around looking for anything that made sense—my phone, makeup remover, a cup of coffee. My phone showed up first, littered with concerned messages from Axel. I wrote him back first, bleary-eyed as I punched out my message with one eye pinched shut. The leftover gunk from my mascara made things difficult.

AXEL: You're scaring me babe. I never miss a chance to say goodnight to you.

CORA: I fell asleep early and slept hard. Must have needed it!

AXEL: It's that new ring, isn't it? Too heavy, makes you tired.

CORA: Yeah, but still gonna need a new one come our wedding day.

AXEL: Working on it. Now what's the big news from last night?

At least there was Axel. The consistent bright spot in my life. The levity and perspective I could count on. He'd picked my sad ass up too many times to count through college. I didn't want to be the perpetually grieving girlfriend, though. I didn't want to get into the nitty-gritty of the letter. I just wanted this issue to lay low for a while.

Which was how I'd been treating it since the beginning.

CORA: Wasn't much of anything. Just some structural concerns about the business. Not worth the bar visit at all.

AXEL: It's because you were with me. He's tracking you. Probably me, too.

Anxiety returned, blossoming in sickening tendrils through my belly. Had my father been reading my text messages all along, too?

CORA: Time for my own cell plan?

AXEL: I'll add you to mine.

AXEL: No, let's get a new plan.

AXEL: For the Fairchild family.

Talking to Axel helped wake me up, restore some clarity. Next order of business: admire my engagement ring. I slipped it back onto my finger, smiling as I went into the bathroom and got cleaned up. After a quick shower and facial scrub, I was ready to return to LA.

I got my things packed up, dressed in a comfy slouchy sweater and jeans, slipped my feet into my favorite flats, and switched my things into my cross-body bag from Venice Beach, storing the designer bag in my carryon.

When I left my room, the smell of eggs and toast wafted through the air. I found my parents in the kitchen where their cook, Geri, whipped up the food I smelled. Perfectly plated avocado toast awaited me.

"Good morning, everyone," I said, forcing a small smile. Geri greeted me more enthusiastically than anyone.

"You look bright and beautiful," she enthused.

"I don't exactly feel it, but thank you."

"I wanted to pack a powerful punch for your flight today, so we're loading up on good fats. I drizzled a freshly made cashew-chipotle sauce on top. The sprouts are radish and pea."

"It looks perfect." I slid onto a high stool facing the center island where Geri had her breakfast station set up. My father lifted a brow from the dinette, where he and my mother sat.

"Care to join us?" my father asked.

"Yes, of course." My gaze dropped to the eggs. "Can you load me up a plate of those too? Extra micro greens. And that cashew whatever. Actually let's just mix it all together."

Geri did as I asked, handing over the large breakfast bowl. I joined my parents at the dinette and saw question marks in my mother's eyes.

"When did you start eating eggs?" she asked.

"Am I not allowed to eat eggs?" I arranged my napkin on my lap as I'd been taught. Even at a casual breakfast, our silverware was precisely arranged, cloth napkins at the ready, everything in place. "I thought that's why they were there."

My mother pursed her lips, her gaze flicking toward Geri. A warning not to stray too far out of line, even in front of the paid help. Signing non-disclosure agreements was standard practice for employees of our family, but we all knew they talked amongst themselves. No NDA clause could eradicate gossip.

"You've always preferred lighter breakfasts." My mother sniffed, her gaze falling to the steaming mug of green tea in front of her—the only breakfast she'd had for the past two and a half decades of being married to my father. "Wouldn't want you to get sick on the plane."

I blinked down at the glorious ensemble in my bowl. It was true—I hadn't eaten eggs growing up. But mostly it had been due to the implicitly suggested lighter everything that my mother thought was appropriate for girls like me. Just a few calories shy of an eating disorder.

"I've been working on a new diet with my trainer out in LA," I told her, which was only partly true. Really it was because my visit to meet Axel's adoptive parents in Kentucky a year ago that had opened my eyes to the joys of fresh-laid eggs for breakfast. They'd showered me in fluffy, cheesy, hens-raised-right-there goodness. Instantly converted. "We're doing three days a week heavy breakfasts to prep for strength training."

"Hm." My mother's practiced face of mild disbelief could have been a meme. "Sounds rigorous."

"It's been great. New regimen, new me," I teased.

"Just don't bulk up too much," my mother said between sips of her tea. "You don't want to confuse Eli."

My nostrils flared as I swallowed the competing reactions that threatened to surface. I wasn't even sure where to begin. "Mother—I...Wow."

"What?" She set her tea down, stage blinking. She was so good at playing the innocent card after the most jagged-edged barbs.

I cleared my throat, stabbing my fork repeatedly into my eggs. Comments like these made me never want to come home. If it hadn't been for Axel, I wouldn't have come this time. Emotion clamped down on my throat as a painful rush of memories swarmed me. Always *feeling like this* around my parents. Despite it all, I kept my face neutral. They couldn't catch a hint of emotion or my father would be on me like bees on honey.

Because the faults in our family had always been crystal clear: Chris had been too queer; I was too emotional.

"I hardly think you need to be that dramatic," I said when I was sure my voice wouldn't betray the landslide of emotions that had pummeled my insides. "It's literally eggs. Just in case, I'll wear a nametag for Eli so he remembers my role within the business."

My mother huffed, something between a harrumph and a laugh. I had to be skilled at needling her anymore, and that one had hit the mark.

"Did you have a chance to read the letter last night?" my father asked, his eyes on Geri as she moved around the kitchen.

I swallowed a forkful of eggs. "I did."

A long silence followed. Their gazes burned on me.

"Difficult to read, to say the least," I finally added and took a bite of my avocado toast. The movement of my left hand with my toast snagged my mother's attention. Her pupils dilated as her gaze connected with the ring on my left hand.

Shit.

I'd forgotten about the engagement ring.

Shit shit shit.

My heart rate quadrupled, and I almost choked on my toast as the tension drew tighter between us.

"Ooh. Honey. What's the newest flair?" Her pinched smile looked strained as she brought the mug of tea to her lips once more. My father's gaze finally landed on the glittering ring. I cursed myself for the oversight. Cursed the brain fog that had allowed me to wander out of my bedroom with the ring in plain sight.

I'd planned to tell them. Just not *now*. Not on the heels of the letter. Not when I didn't have my plan in place.

"I didn't realize you'd gone shopping while you've been here," my father muttered.

"It looks like an engagement ring," my mother said on the heels of a fluttery laugh.

I couldn't lie about this. "It is."

My mother's eyes flashed wide for the briefest of moments before she swung her gaze toward my father. He shifted, the wood chair creaking.

"Geri, can you please give us a moment?" my father asked, his eyes lasered in on me. A forest sage tempest swirled there.

"Of course! I'll pop these muffins in the oven when I get back," she said, wiping her hands on a towel as she dutifully left the kitchen. My parents waited a few moments after Geri left before launching the assault.

"Who gave you that ring?" My father's schooled voice couldn't hide the quake of anger.

"Axel," I whispered so quietly I almost couldn't hear myself.

"Why are you even still seeing him?" my mother hissed, as though Geri lurked within hearing distance.

My mouth flopped open and closed a few times before I said, "He's my boyfriend. My fiancé now."

"What she means to say," my father spit out, "is why would you throw away your future on a boy like him?"

"I'm not throwing my future away," I replied, but my voice withered in the face of their outrage.

"There is no future with him," my father said, his fingers curling into a tight fist. "If you are with him, you've thrown it all away. It's as simple as that, Cora."

"I don't understand why you see it like that," I whispered. The tears had returned, the emotion clamping my throat, and this time I wasn't strong enough to will any trace away. "He's a good man. He's destined for greatness. He's—"

"He's nothing," my father repeated. "He's a joke. He's a-a-a passing fancy."

"Something you need to get out of your system," my mother said in a low voice. "Which is what you're doing, right?"

"I don't want him out of my system," I said faintly. I wasn't sure I had the strength to weather this conversation after the torment of reading Chris's letter. But this conversation had to happen. "I want to marry him."

My father laughed bitterly, shaking his head as if I'd suggested I wanted to marry a lamp post. "You absolutely will not."

"I will," I said, though it was so quiet I wasn't sure I had really said it.

My mother pressed two fingers to the center of her forehead. "You'll get this out of your system. And then you will come to your senses."

"No daughter of mine is marrying a…a hillbilly like that," my father sputtered. "You were bred for better things than what he can offer you. We didn't give you everything you needed on a silver fucking platter just for you to throw it all away on a piece of redneck trash like him."

The tears had arrived, and they did not care about keeping quiet. A sob ratcheted my chest. "He's not trash. If you'd get to know him—"

"I know enough," my father hissed. "He's got nothing. He can offer you nothing. How can you not see this, Cora?"

"Please. Come to your senses," my mother said quietly, reaching out to squeeze my wrist. The motherly gesture felt like a rebuke. I snatched my hand away and tried to swallow another sob. Silence scraped by, eternal and coarse between the three of us. I covered my face with my hands, trying like hell to compose myself.

"Stop crying," my mother said after a moment. "There's no need to be so emotional."

Her words were both a warning and a plea. In this family, there was never any need to be emotional. Not even when my parents were ripping my heart out of my chest and forcing me to watch myself bleed out.

My instinct was to apologize, to quiet myself, to return to stone as they wanted. And I tried. I tried so hard. I'd been practicing this my entire life. But the pain of what they'd voiced here was too great.

I was still nursing the wounds Chris's letter had reopened, and now they wanted me to stick a knife into my chest and act like it didn't hurt.

"You need to do what's best for your future," my father went on. "You can't let your emotions get in the way. How do you think we built this family to such great heights? Not by letting our hearts fuck everything up."

"There is a time and a place for love," my mother interjected. "And this is not it."

"Frankly, I thought we taught you better than that," my father sniffed. The disappointment in his voice prompted another pummeling wave of tears that I fought like hell to obscure.

"Maybe you should just go," my mother finally said when my attempts to stop crying were unsuccessful. She checked her watch. "You might be late. Allan, let's call the car."

My father grunted and pulled out his phone. I drew a ragged breath, dabbing at my eyes with my napkin.

My mother tutted. "You're getting mascara on the napkin."

I set the napkin down, swiping my fingers across my cheeks. This conversation was far from finished, but nothing else would come from this for now. "I'll go get my things."

"The car will be here shortly," my father announced, as breezily as though we'd just ended a business meeting. I nodded, excusing myself to go back to my bedroom so I could regroup, drawing deep, cleansing breaths.

But the truth was nothing would fully cleanse me of the disgust and disdain that had poured out of them.

They detested Axel because he wasn't their kind. Not their kind of person and not their kind of money.

And no amount of time, tears, or conversation would ever help us find common ground.

CHAPTER TEN

CORA

Back in LA, I drifted onward, listless and blank. I couldn't even bring myself to tell Axel about the encounter with my parents. I didn't want him to worry—or maybe I just didn't want him to probe. There were too many big unanswered questions, and all I knew how to do for now was look away. I had no emotional bandwidth left to dive into the quagmire.

Because it wasn't just about Axel. It was about Chris's hopes, too. He'd wanted me to take over the family business, a position that had been designated for him. He'd wanted nothing more than to make our father proud, up to and including denying his own sexuality. And if there was anything I wanted in life, it was to honor my brother's truth. The truth he sought to squash and mute. The guilt that I carried from his suicide was a poison that had been dissolving my insides for years. Joining the family business was a way to atone. I could still live the life that Chris had always dreamt for us.

But I couldn't turn away from Axel.

There had to be a way to blend the two paths. I just didn't know what it was.

Monday morning, after a day and a half of tense expectation waiting for the other shoe to drop, they called.

"Cora, we're both here," my mother announced after I'd picked up, her voice bland and hollow. "Are you available to chat?"

"Of course," I said, setting my purse down in the front hallway of my condo. I'd just gotten back from seminar and an immaculate home greeted me. The housekeeper had come and gone during the morning, leaving everything exactly as I liked it—including a bowl of mints near the door for guests.

"Good. We need to get some things clear moving forward," my father said brusquely.

"About what?" I asked unnecessarily. Like this conversation could be about anything other than the engagement ring still encircling my finger.

"About your involvement with the family," he said.

Ouch. Emotion clamped my throat straight away this time. At least they weren't there to see the hurt that had begun stretching itself through my limbs.

"Oh. I didn't realize my status as a family member was up for debate."

"Everything is up for debate, at all times," my father said. "Another thing I thought you'd learned by now."

"Well, let's hear it." I clutched the phone so tightly my knuckles ached. "Let's hear the new rules."

"There are no new rules," he went on. "There is simply a choice. By now I think it is apparent that your mother and I want the best for you. We've worked tirelessly our entire lives to offer you the best of the best of everything. You have a personal driver on each coast. You have residences on each coast. Housekeepers, paid schooling, private chefs, personal trainers, a limitless allowance for whatever your heart desires. We are prepared to finance your lifestyle for as long as you require. But that financing only happens if certain conditions are met."

The knot that had been tightening in my stomach now cinched into a sickening stone.

"I think it's also clear how we feel about this boy you insist on calling your boyfriend," my father added. "But in case there was any doubt, I'll reiterate: he is a neanderthal. We refuse to be associated with someone whose name sounds better suited for the car mechanic he should have become. We would never do business with him, and we certainly will not allow someone like him to become part of our family."

I made a small noise, but my mother interjected. "Whatever you're feeling now for him, I promise, it will pass. You will survive without him. I swear it."

"The key words being *without him*," my father said gruffly. "Because we will not allow him to become part of this empire. Your future does not include him, if you wish to continue in this family."

Tears streamed down my cheeks, but I held back the sobs threatening to escape.

"Continue in this family?" I echoed. "So if I stay with Axel I'll no longer be your daughter?" I laughed bitterly. "That's insane."

"Empire and family are one and the same."

"So why don't you invite the board members to our birthdays?" I shot back.

"Don't start splitting hairs," my mother warned.

"If you continue with this boy, you'll have none of the conveniences you've come to expect at your disposal," my father said with the air of someone discussing an upcoming business trip. "You'll be on your own. All credit cards, drivers, housekeepers, trainers, allowances, and air travel will be revoked."

Silence pounded the air around me. My father had more; I could feel it in the tense stretch of miles between us, tugging tight like the promise of a bungee cord at the bottom of the ravine.

"I don't understand," I whispered. "What does it matter? I'll step up for the company. I'll work with Eli. Just let me be with Axel."

"Absolutely not."

"We'll keep it a secret," I said, the emotion making my voice come out strained and swollen. "Nobody has to know."

"Oh, Cora, don't be so daft," my mother chided. "You're in business school. Act like it."

"You cannot have it both ways," my father went on. "Because if you choose him, you are choosing failure. I will not permit that boy to be associated with my brand. With my livelihood. With everything I have fought my entire life to create, maintain, and uphold. If he is in any way associated with the Margulis name, I will make sure that he sinks."

"What does that mean?" I asked, forcing my voice to be steady when everything inside me was crumbling.

"It means whatever it needs to mean. You stay away from him, and he is free to pursue his bad ideas with his own agenda in his own ways. But if he dares comes near my empire? I'm prepared to do whatever is necessary to ensure he doesn't even touch the ground I spit on. Do you understand?"

I swiped at some tears that had fallen. "If I choose him and you ruin him, then you're ruining me too."

"So you do understand." An eternal pause. "But if this man is so important to you, I'm sure that will be a small sacrifice," my father said, the sarcasm dripping through the cell connection.

"I don't understand why he's so incompatible," I finally forced out. "I know he doesn't come from money." I swallowed the hiccup of a sob that threatened to out my careening emotions. "But he's driven. Just like you were."

"His drive is laughable. Besides, this role requires you have an appropriate partner at your side," my father said. "And the joke of a man you're currently choosing is definitely *not* appropriate."

"He's not a joke," I forced out, moving down the hallway on leaden legs. "Just because he's adopted doesn't mean he's worse."

"He's utterly inferior in every conceivable way." My father's voice came out a menacing hiss. "You don't know what you're getting into. I can share the police reports if you're interested. The adoption records. The bankruptcy filings from his adoptive parents. Which documents would you like to peruse first?"

The weight of this conversation had forced me to sink down the side of the wall. I brought my knees to my chest, crying into my knees.

"You just have to make a choice." My mother's voice cracked, the first ounce of emotion I'd heard from her since the start of this conversation. "Choose your future."

"You don't have to answer now," my father added. "Take your time to think about it, because once you choose, there is no turning back. This is an irrevocable decision. Life is full of hard choices, Cora. But choosing correctly is what separates the winners from the losers. We've groomed you to be a winner. To be the best of the best. There's a reason you are where you are right now. And I don't think you want to skydive from your golden perch right now, because you will hit the ground hard. You're not ready to confront the reality of what awaits you at the bottom."

"Think about it," my mother repeated. "Please."

"We'll need an answer by Friday," my father said. And then the line went dead.

My cell phone clattered to the floor, and I covered my face with my hands while the sobs rolled out of me. I hadn't ever felt so profoundly trampled or betrayed by my family. Being with Axel had always been risky, but I'd never imagined they'd threaten my status as a family member. This felt like royal exile, worse than when Prince Harry stepped down.

It wasn't the potential loss of the creature comforts that worried me. While I sat in the front hallway, crying and imagining the future without my driver or chef or trainer, I was confident I could hack it. My father might not believe in me, but who did he really believe in except himself? Sure, it would take some getting used to. I had never even really looked at my monthly budget before, but I could start, see what I could whittle down.

With Axel at my side, we could take it on. We could start our new reality. We would start our new business and be fine, just like Axel had always said.

But if I chose him, then I'd be ruining Axel's future too. Axel was set on Fairchild Enterprises becoming a premier investment firm. He and his brothers could move to Mongolia, and my father would still be able to block them at every turn. My father's reach, and network, was incredibly far-reaching.

And there wasn't anything Axel wanted more than to make something of himself. To shoot for the stars and hit the next galaxy over, as he'd always said. If I took that away from him, the guilt would eat me alive.

Chris's letter lingered unpleasantly in my thoughts.

This was my chance to honor him. To give him what he wanted for our family, that sparkling best-case scenario that he'd seen as the ultimate goal, even in his darkest moments.

I hadn't helped Chris enough while he was alive. The only way I could redeem myself was to give him what he wanted for the Margulis family.

Choosing for Chris created my personal worst-case scenario.

Choosing for Axel created his personal worst-case scenario.

There was no winning here. Not for me. Not for anyone.

CHAPTER ELEVEN

AXEL

"You want Chinese tonight or Korean?" Damian asked dully from the kitchen as he rustled through take-out menus.

"We got enough money for takeout again?" Trace asked sharply from the bathroom, where he was shaving in front of the tiny mirror.

"We fucking better," I chimed in as I opened the refrigerator, assessing the absolutely abysmal state of anything edible. "Because it's not looking so hot in here."

"This is where we should try an activity called 'going to the store,'" Trace said, tapping his razor against the side of the sink. He had a big interview tomorrow with a potential employer since he was graduating this semester, instead of next semester like Damian and me. Somehow after almost a decade of practice, he still sucked at shaving. He needed some time to let the nicks heal before meeting with these people. "I know it sounds like a drag, but I promise you we can make our own food on occasion. Mom might not have wanted us in the kitchen often, but we all know how to boil some damn noodles and make a solid Bolognese sauce."

"So...does that mean get groceries delivered?" I asked Damian.

"Jesus. You guys suck at managing money," Trace muttered.

"That's why you'll be CFO of our business," I shot back. "We know you're the best, Mr. Money God. Now should we waste time ordering groceries and cooking, or just have them bring the Chicken Teriyaki straight to our mouths like we want?"

Trace sighed dramatically.

"Chicken teriyaki," Damian confirmed. The food debate was resolved, but the money worries tugged at me. We'd been skating the line with destitution for a few weeks. What had been a declined debit card the night I proposed to Cora was actually an overdrawn bank account and now, a late tuition payment. Luckily, one of our favorite Chinese places accepted cryptocurrency, which meant we could eat for at least a couple more months on our crypto holdings alone.

"I'll make sausage and potatoes next week," I called over my shoulder to Trace. "Just like Mom's. Promise."

He grumbled something I didn't hear as he rinsed off his razor. Tiny bits of toilet paper dotted his chin and left cheek as he came out into the kitchen.

"Another shave well done," I teased him. "You're ready for the work force, buddy, you walking cube steak."

"Fuck off," he said. "You guys know as well as I do that I need this job so we can all stay afloat and launch our business like it deserves. If I were you, I'd be offering to shave this beautiful mug myself just to woo the recruiter."

I clapped him on the back. "That sounds like one of your weirdo fantasies again."

"Is this the part where we're supposed to thank you for graduating early and taking care of your broke brothers?" Damian deadpanned. "Because if it is, you'll have to inform the class of your expectations."

"I think we should just go ahead and give him the accolades anyway," I told Damian. "That way he'll be more willing to support us once he makes his first billion and we're still trying to graduate."

Trace blinked. "I'm honored you think I could make a billion dollars that fast."

"Or maybe I was saying that it'll take Damian and me a few more years to finish this shit up."

We all shared warm smiles. The playful ribbing was one of our tried-and-true methods for dealing with money anxiety. We'd learned during our teenage years, once Damian and I had really gotten settled at the Fairchild house. It had taken us about a year to feel safe enough to let the Fairchilds into our hearts and three more before we completed the formal adoption process and traded the last name Haynes for Fairchild.

The home we found with Deb and Gary Fairchild was warm but cash strapped. Trace was their only biological kid, and the addition of two foster brothers made for a bustling but broke household. Even if my younger sisters hadn't been split up from us before the Fairchilds, they certainly wouldn't have been able to join us, and their loss still haunted me.

I'd spent years traumatized by and rehashing the turn of events that split us up from our two sisters. When we found out that Kaylee had passed away our freshman year of college, it only made everything sting worse. She'd become a victim of human trafficking. The same system that failed her had uplifted us. We still couldn't find Jordan. We'd been able to find out that she and Kaylee had been separated at some point after their initial joint placement. It hurt too bad to consider where—or how—she might have ended up. Especially when Damian and I were thriving. Where was the fucking balance in that?

Yet despite those first tumultuous years in the foster care system, Damian and I found some stability. We saw that a decent future was possible. We scooped horse shit for a meager allowance while Mama Deb and Papa Gary lightened the money stress load with a rotating repertoire of jokes and lightheartedness. We were one emergency away from the food pantry, but it never felt that serious.

It wasn't until we got out on our own that we realized how fucking poor we really were.

I swiped at my phone, ready to order some damn chicken teriyaki but also half-looking for a sign of life from Cora. Since she'd left, something had been off. Even three weeks later, she still wouldn't tell me what, but I felt it, and I searched for some way to equalize the pressure. The only way I knew how was to get my ass out to LA and visit her, but after buying the engagement ring and stocking the apartment with toilet paper, we were tapped.

AXEL: Hey babe. Haven't heard from you since this morning. How are classes? I wish I could squeeze you right now.

She'd been taking longer to write back, which she blamed on her classes. And the longer she took to write back, the more I needed to hear from her, which made me feel like a codependent twatwaffle. I watched the message thread for a moment and then turned the screen off.

"What's wrong?" Damian asked quietly at my side. He'd started thumbing through the takeout menu from the Chinese restaurant that accepted Bitcoin.

"Nothing."

"Oh, okay. Then why do you look like you're trying to shit out a screwdriver?"

I blinked, looking over at him in surprise. "Have you ever shit out a screwdriver?"

Trace looked up at us from across the kitchen island that doubled as our dining room table. "What did Cora do to you with a screwdriver?"

I X'd my hands through the air. "Let's back it up. There were no screwdrivers involved, unless Damian had a farm accident back in the day he forgot to tell us about."

"Okay, so what's wrong?" Damian tried again.

"Nothing," I repeated.

"Then let me rephrase." He paused, licking his lips in thought. "How's Cora?"

My gut twisted. Fuck my brothers for knowing me so well. "She's fine, I guess."

"You guess," Trace echoed. "That sounds weird, coming from you. I thought you guys were telepathically connected."

"The telepathy only works when she uses her phone, which she's doing less of these days." I worked my jaw back and forth. I hated how my brothers could tease the truth out of me so fucking fast. "I dunno. Something's been different since she left, and I can't figure out what it is."

"You sure it isn't pre-wedding jitters?" Damian asked.

"I'm sure. I've never been more certain of anything in my life, actually. But I swear to God Cora is just...distant."

"But she said yes," Trace reminded me. "She wants to marry you."

"I know," I said, though I didn't know. I felt like this entire house of cards could crumble at any time. Not just with Cora, but with what we were trying to do out here. With the business. With all of it. "Maybe she realized how broke I am and wised up."

"I'm pretty sure she's always known how broke you are," Damian teased.

"Yeah, but dating a broke guy is different from marrying one."

"She's not like that," Trace reassured me. "I know she isn't. You know she isn't. You guys have been together for three years. She's probably just stressed from school."

"Yeah, you're right," I muttered, running my fingers through the front of my hair. I wanted to believe him so badly, but I just didn't. "I honestly expected some kind of blowback by now from her dad. I guess she hasn't told him yet."

"He'll find out come the wedding day," Damian laughed.

"Can't wait for the suit fitting," Trace said, shoving my shoulder. "Where we gonna have the bachelor party?"

I smirked. "Depends on if you're bankrolling this shit or not."

"Of course. Anything for my younger brother," Trace said, touching his palm to his heart.

"Does that apply to me too?" Damian asked.

"You have to actually want to get married first," Trace shot back. "And, you know, date someone."

Damian frowned, looking at the takeout menu in his hands. His glasses slipped down his nose, and he pushed them back up with his index finger. "I've dated plenty."

"You've *fucked around* plenty, which is not the same as dating," Trace said.

While my brothers continued splitting hairs about fucking vs. dating, I swiped my phone open again. I returned to my thread with Cora, realizing the last time she'd written to me that day had been at nine a.m., and it was six o'clock now. My stomach plummeted to the floor all over again.

I called her immediately. This wasn't right.

The phone rang and rang while my brothers continued bickering about the virtues of fuck buddies. Arguing in our family was just another way to show love. The call clicked over to voicemail. I hung up and shot off another text to Cora.

AXEL: Babe, is everything okay? You've been distant and it's making me worried.

I got my brothers back on track then and we ordered our Chinese food, forking over miniscule amounts of crypto in exchange for the hot and greasy delivery. Just as the food arrived forty minutes later, I got a call from an unknown number in Los Angeles.

"Hello?" I answered, half of me expecting it to be a telemarketer, the other half expecting it to be a bill collector.

"Axel, thank god you picked up." It was Cora. Relief flooded me, fast and hot. I nearly toppled from the sensation.

"Babe, where have you been? What's wrong? What number is this?"

"I'm using my friend's phone. I'm sorry I haven't texted. My phone's been acting weird."

I snapped my fingers. It was just the phone. Everything was fine. At least, I wanted to believe that. "You had me worried you were dead."

She laughed, but it sounded sad, like I'd told a joke and wasn't aware of it. "No, everything is fine."

Silence blossomed between us. I had so many questions for her I didn't know where to start.

"How was your day?" I finally asked.

"It was fine. Long. Stressful." From the background, I heard someone say "Eli, what's up!" The hairs of my forearms stood at attention.

"And what are you up to now?"

"At a meeting with some classmates," she said. There were some cheers in the background.

It was so noisy, wherever she was, that I could hardly even think of what I wanted to talk to her about. It wasn't the place for us to connect or catch up like we needed to. "Can you call me when you get home?"

"If my phone works," she said.

"Do you need me to send you a new one?"

"I'm getting it figured out."

I worked my jaw back and forth as I mulled over her words. Something was wrong. Just a little off, like chatting with someone who was posing as Cora.

"Hey, I better get going," she said. "I love you, Axel. Talk soon."

The line was dead before I could even return the words. I frowned as I pocketed the phone and reached for my takeout container. Chicken teriyaki awaited me, and my grumbling stomach was ready.

"So, she called you," Trace said as he slurped some beef lo mein past his lips. "That's good."

"Yeah. Except she didn't use her phone and she was with Eli."

"Eli?" Damian asked, hunched over his orange chicken.

"The rich douchebag her parents want her to marry." I stabbed at my food, the aromas not exciting me like they normally did. I shoved a forkful of chicken into my mouth. After chewing thoughtfully, I added, "I think I need to go out there."

"To LA?" Damian asked.

"No, to Shanghai." I kicked his leg in the armchair next to me. "Yes, LA."

"They sell plane tickets with crypto yet?" Trace cracked.

"No." I stabbed my chopsticks into my food again and then caught Trace's eye. "Was thinking maybe you could sell off a share or two for me."

Trace let out an exaggerated groan. "You've gotta be kidding me."

"Dude, something is wrong with Cora. We just need to *see* each other, you know? It's probably her dad making shit weird somehow. I mean, isn't it always? He's probably tracking her. I dunno—I just need to see her."

"I know you miss your girlfriend—" Trace started.

"Fiancée," I corrected sharply.

"Right, your fiancée. But that doesn't justify selling off shares so you can afford a plane ticket." Trace dipped his head, sending me an admonishing look from over his takeout container. He managed the family fortune, as I liked to call it. Really, it was an expertly diversified portfolio of stocks, bonds, and more that Trace managed and grew for us so we could reap the dividends each quarter. It was one of the main reasons we could stay afloat in Manhattan—his ingenuity. "We have to be smart. We're on limited resources until I get this job or we snag a few early clients for our business."

"But something is wrong. I know it is." I took another bite of food, unnerved by how bland I found it. That alone was a sign that something needed to be done. "I can't explain it."

"I think you've got the jitters," Damian offered.

"Fuck your jitters," I told him. "Cora and I, we're connected, okay?" I stabbed angrily at a piece of chicken and then realized I actually wasn't hungry anymore. I set the container down and leaned back on the couch, interlocking my fingers across my forehead. "She's been acting weird since she left. And I've gotta figure out why."

The thing about grad school was that it sucked. The days were long, and the money struggles were real. That didn't even take into account my internship, which paid just enough to skirt labor laws. But even with how much was going on in my day-to-day, I could still count the accumulating absences of Cora.

They piled up in the lengthy response times, seconds stacked on minutes stacked on entire days. They sliced at me with each unanswered call. The short, abnormally stilted calls with Cora, like the night of the crypto chicken teriyaki, started happening more and more. I even sent flowers to her house once, got the delivery confirmation, and she didn't mention them for two entire days. Sometimes, she'd message me from inside a social media app for the first time in a day. Who the fuck did stuff like that after three years together and an engagement?

Not my Cora. The more time that trudged by, the worse I felt about it. She always dodged the distance comment. No matter how many times I mentioned the distance growing like a chasm between us, she'd deflect, divert, or hang up.

I felt like I was engaged to a shadow, the wisps of which disappeared anytime I happened to catch a glimpse.

And as far as I was concerned, it wasn't going to continue like this. The semester was almost over, which meant Cora should be coming home for the holidays soon. But I hadn't heard a peep out of her about it. A week before Christmas, I decided enough was enough. I'd get her to open up. To stop stressing about classes—if that's what this really was—or take a chill pill or whatever she needed to do.

AXEL: Call me ASAP. Very important.

I sent the message through the last random social media app she'd used to message me and waited. I waited all fucking day, in fact. I spent the entire day bouncing between the business and economics library and my exams scattered around campus. This was the second-to-last exam period I'd ever have in my life—wasn't that incredible—but I could barely enjoy how close I was to getting my MBA because all I could think about was Cora.

I finally got a call from a random ass LA number around eight p.m. It had to be her. Because this was normal now.

"Cora?" I asked as I picked up.

"Axel. Hey. What's up?"

I peered around the walls of my library study cubby. I couldn't have this conversation here. They'd shush me out of the damn building. I bolted for the stairwell, keeping my voice low. "Just finishing up some studying for my last exam. How are you?"

Her pause said more than her words. "I'm okay."

"Are you?" I pushed out into the stairwell, a gust of cool, paper-tinged air whooshing around me.

"Of course. Why wouldn't I be?"

I expelled a breath I'd been holding. "Because you're acting super fucking weird these days."

When she remained quiet, I realized it was because she didn't even have a way to defend herself. So she recognized it too.

"What's going on with you, babe?" I asked softly. My fingers twitched from wanting to see her. Hold her. Soothe her. "You've got me worried."

"I don't know." Her voice sounded a million miles away. "I don't know, Axel."

"Well, can we fix this?" I leaned against the wall, staring through the thick, square window in the stairwell door, back into the library proper. Inside there, everything was orderly. Organized. The opposite of the majority of my childhood. It represented the pinnacle of everything I'd fought for alongside my brothers. But here in the stairwell, my entire world threatened to unravel. Whatever Cora said during this phone call had the power to demolish everything.

She'd always had that power, because I'd willingly ceded it to her. She was the only woman in the world who would ever get it.

Cora was quiet for a while, which grated on me.

"Cora," I snapped. "What is going on? You need to talk to me."

"I am."

"Oh, is this what you call talking?" I scoffed, fisting the front of my hair. "You used to open up to me, no problem. Do you even still want to marry me?"

She gasped. "Axel! How could you just—" She sighed heatedly. "That's a leap and you know it."

"It's an honest question. Do you want to?"

"You know the answer."

Her evasiveness was infuriating. My blood pumped faster, hotter, angrier. "Why can't you give me a yes or a no?"

"Axel," she started, but nothing else followed.

"Here, let me show you how it sounds. Cora, I am deeply invested in our relationship. I would kill another human being to keep you in my life. Your happiness is literally more important than my own. The only thing I want to do more than launch this business with my brothers is become your husband and have kids with you."

Silence flooded the line, but it wasn't long before I caught the muffled hiccup of a sob.

"Cora, what the fuck is going on with you?" I shouted, my voice echoing in the stairwell. The double doors swung open then, two students eyeballing me as they headed downward.

"Things have been weird around here, Axel," she said, her voice thick with emotion.

"It's your dad."

"It's more than that," she whispered.

"I can't help you if you don't talk to me. Babe, we need a beach session."

"Now?"

"Yes. Emergency beach meeting." The beach meetings always put us right. Searching for the beach glass that resembled each other's eye color calmed in a way nothing else could. I knew that if we had a shot at fixing this, it would happen on the beach. The Hamptons were a trek and a half from where I stood right now, but I'd go, even if it took me until midnight.

"I can't."

"What? Then let's do it tomorrow."

"No, I...I can't." Her voice was thick with tears.

The rejection was so stunning I grappled for air for a moment. "Okay. Then when are you coming home? It's almost Christmas. Let's just go together when you're back."

"I'm not coming home this year. My parents have already flown out to LA for Christmas. I—" Her voice faltered but she didn't pick up her train of thought. I mulled over her words. If her parents were out there, then they were probably putting a lot of pressure on her.

"Did they find out about the engagement?"

"Yes."

"Jesus, Cora, why didn't you tell me?" I slapped my palm against the smooth wall, creating a loud *bang!* "That's news, you know? That's some fucking news you should share with me."

"I haven't had a chance," she said, her voice watery again. "I-I-I've been so busy."

"Busy? I—" My voice faltered as a tidal wave of emotion swept through me. "Clearly. You're so busy you can't even talk to your fiancé. How are we gonna make a marriage work if you can't even talk to me while we're engaged?"

"Axel, you're just...*doing it* again," she hissed.

"Doing what?"

"You're being overbearing."

"You think that me wanting to talk to my *fiancée* is overbearing?"

"I think you do a lot of things in a really overbearing way," she snapped.

"Wow. This is just—wow. I don't even have the words."

Tense silence settled between us.

"It's like pulling teeth to get you on the phone anymore," I blurted. "I'm shocked we aren't messaging on Instagram right now, since that's apparently where you love to conduct our relationship now."

"Axel—"

"I never thought I'd see the day when you'd have to resort to social media to talk to me. I could solve this right now and send you a phone, but no. That's not good enough. Why don't you tell me what's really going on, Cora?"

Her voice was thick with tears. "I think we should take a break."

I stared at the wall in front of me for so long I forgot where I was. But the double doors opening for other students reminded me.

"Excuse me?"

"I-I...You heard me."

"I just asked you to marry me, and you've got cold feet already?"

"Yes."

"After three years together?"

"Axel—"

"Why didn't you just send me a message on Instagram?"

She sighed shakily, quiet sobs escaping her.

"This is bullshit. I'm flying out there so we can have this conversation in person." I fisted the front of my hair, my heart rate near fatal levels. I wanted to cry and break my phone and punch the cement wall into pieces all at the same time. None of this made sense. Not a fucking bit of it.

"You can't," she said. "My dad is here."

"I don't fucking care. What does he matter?"

"Don't come," she warned in a low voice. "It won't end well."

"Oh, and you asking for a break from two thousand miles away is the happy ending you dreamed of? Cora, what the fuck is wrong? Seriously—are you ill? Do you have a brain tumor?"

A soft laugh made it past the tears, but it was sadder than I'd ever heard.

"You yourself told me that your father did not matter when it came to making our future work," I spat into the phone. A couple students slowed as they walked by me, and I glared at them before whipping around to stare at a different part of the wall. "Why does he matter now? The only reason I can think of for you breaking up with me is that he put you up to it."

"He didn't," she said after a pause. "This is my decision. I think this is what is best." More sobs rolled out of her. "I'm allowed to have second thoughts."

"Second thoughts."

"Yes. I've been thinking about what I want and I just..."

"You what?"

She sniffed. "You're too much. I can't even function when I'm around you. Seeing you and then not being with you and then—the future—I just—" She was blubbering then, like she'd been reading notes and dropped them halfway through.

"I don't believe this for a second." She sounded like a robot. Like a half-dead impersonation of the woman I loved. "You're acting crazy, but we can talk this out. If nothing else, you need a welfare check."

"I'm fine," she insisted with a tear-clogged voice.

"Yeah. You sound real fine."

She whimpered. "I have to go."

The line went dead, and I stared at my phone for a few moments, asking myself if I was really awake. Maybe this was part of an active nightmare. Something I'd slipped into due to exams.

But when I accessed my call history, the ten-minute conversation was on the top line.

This shit was real. And my world was officially falling the fuck apart.

I gathered my shit and raced out of the library.

Trace wouldn't be happy with me, but I needed to cash out my stocks.

I wouldn't take no for an answer. Not when I needed to get to LA yesterday.

CHAPTER TWELVE

CORA

The ringing of my phone in the other room sent another wave of nausea through me.

I dragged myself off the couch and stumbled toward the downstairs bathroom.

Anxiety puke number five for the week: Check.

As I wiped off my face and braced myself to pick up my phone, another wave of dread washed through me. It had been one of few constants these days, along with utter confusion and profound loss.

Not to mention deep, penetrating sadness.

The decision I'd made to follow the path Chris—and my father—wanted for me came at a steep cost. Not only forsaking the man I loved, but uprooting my entire life as I knew it and starting anew.

DAD: The movers will be arriving within ten minutes. Be ready.

I drew a shaky breath. Packers had been in and out of my condo for the past week, prepping everything to be moved. I had barely paid attention except to instruct them to leave the personal things under my bed alone. I'd collected every vestige of Axel there, evidence of the love that my father could never touch, would never erase.

That love would continue for the rest of my life, whether or not I was with Axel.

Because I wasn't just accepting what Chris wanted for me. I was also doing what was best for Axel. How could honoring two men I loved so much feel so absolutely wretched?

I had no hope that this feeling would go away either. My hands were tied. I couldn't tell Axel the whole truth. If I did, he'd fly off the handle. He'd jeopardize his own future. He'd ruin everything he and his brothers had fought for.

Axel would demolish his own existence to rail against my father. And that wouldn't help anyone.

If nothing else, I wanted Axel and his brothers to achieve their dreams. That much, I could give him.

I tried to improve my appearance in the bathroom mirror, but it was mostly pointless. There was no real way to hide the puffiness from crying daily for the past three weeks. Makeup helped my skin look less pallid, but nourishing myself had taken a backseat while I grieved the loss of Axel and struggled to rationalize how I could do this to him. Even my personal chef was getting concerned at how little I ate. I knew they were all reporting back to my parents, but so far, my mother and father hadn't said a word to me about my concerning behavior.

They probably didn't care. Their only concern was that Axel disappear from my life.

And technically, I hadn't quite achieved that. I'd managed to ask for a break two nights ago on the phone, tucked into the closet of a classmate's apartment. Extreme measures were all I had left in my toolbox. My father monitored my phone usage like a hawk, all the way down to who I sent emails to and how long any call with a New York number lasted, lest I be communicating with Axel on the sly.

After my housekeeper had ratted on me using her phone to call Axel, my options had dwindled to social media and telepathy. Two weeks ago, my father had told me that no further communication was permitted. I'd assured him things were over.

Except they weren't. And now Axel was coming to LA.

Highlighting his entire plan via text messages that my father was probably lapping up like honey.

DAD: The driver isn't far behind.

I stumbled into the white-tiled entrance hall of my condo, looking around at the stripped-bare surroundings. All the splashes of color I'd added—from the exciting gold sprays of decorative branches to the black swirl pedestals I'd chosen for my favorite candles—were absent. Packed up. Awaiting a new home, in a new neighborhood. I'd loved this place and had no desire to move.

My father had insisted on new surroundings for me. *A home that better fits the future CEO*, he'd said. But really, it better fit the current CEO. My condo had been on the smaller side, with only two spare bedrooms, neither of which were to my father's standards for visiting overnight. Not that he ever needed to use the condo to stay in, though I think this aspect figured into the decision to upgrade my living space.

This new house cost a cool three million and had double master suites. I suspected my parents planned to claim one for their own – probably so they could keep a better eye on me during their random and frequent visits to the west coast. Located a couple of miles outside of town, the house was tucked into its own private Stanford oasis. Stunning views of the mountains from afar coupled with an in-ground infinity pool that begged me to have a housewarming party.

Except my favorite guest couldn't attend. And by my father's design, that same guest didn't even know where this new home was.

Another wave of sadness gripped me, but I swallowed it when a knock sounded. The movers had arrived. I forced a smile the only way I knew how and shoved aside the emotions that had been holding me hostage for weeks now.

"Ms. Margulis," the man at the door said after consulting his work order. "We're ready when you are."

I would never be ready. Not in my heart. My entire world had brought me to this point, but everything inside me wanted to bolt the other direction.

The only thing keeping me on the path was the fact that I felt like it was the right thing to do. Giving Axel and his brothers the chance to flourish. Choosing the family business. Becoming the CEO my father and my late brother wanted me to be. Following this carefully laid path that had been built, painstakingly, over the years specifically for me. Even if I didn't love it, it was right.

Sometimes the hardest choices are the right choices. I had an ever-growing list of mantras that dotted my waking hours. *You have a legacy to uphold. Nobody said it would be easy.*

I directed the movers as best I could, keeping a close watch on the box of personal items. Knowing my father, I couldn't rule out that he somehow knew the last of Axel's things were tucked away there, including the drawstring baggie of beach glass in the same blue thunderstorm of his eyes.

Once the movers were packing up the last of the truck, I tucked the box under my arm, grabbed my purse, and let Randall, our West Coast driver, whisk me away to my new home.

I'd been there only once before, back when my parents had sent me a long list of potential properties to visit. I'd offered my preferences, but this one hadn't even been in the top three. I could only assume we'd been too slow or bid too low to secure the home I truly wanted.

And really, what did it matter? This was a gift. I could say nothing. Even though I desperately wanted to select a home for myself, even if my choice was drastically smaller and in a different part of town, that wasn't how this transaction worked.

My father made the decisions.

Everything happened according to his liking. To his tastes. To his desires.

And everyone around him just watched as the vice clamped tighter.

"Darling. Welcome to your new home!" My mother was there in the slate-paved cul-de-sac of the two-story stucco home that had once, according to the realtor, been an early residence of Jennifer Aniston. I'd seen Jennifer Aniston in that show *Friends* that Axel had me binge with him on Netflix once, so it was a talking point, if nothing else, for future guests.

"Thanks, Mother." I tried the forced smile again, but it failed to light. My cheeks twitched and gave up.

I hauled myself out of the car, limbs sluggish and heavy.

"Quit slouching," she snapped quietly. "I thought you'd grown out of that after you turned thirteen."

"Must be regressing," I muttered, straightening my back. My body clearly wanted to curl into the fetal position and remain there for a year until I metamorphosed into a different, rested, emotionless version of myself. But until then, slouching was the only thing that made sense.

"Did everything go okay at the old place?"

"Sure. Yeah. Great. It's empty and ready for the next person." I slung my purse over my shoulder and grabbed my box of Axel memorabilia.

"What's in there?"

"Just my personal stuff I don't want the movers touching," I told her. "My earrings and bracelets and whatnot."

My mother sniffed and nodded, already not listening. "I came to help get you settled. This is a big day! Aren't you thrilled?"

Thrilled was not even in the top hundred words I'd use to describe how I felt, so I just said, "Mmm. Yes."

My phone buzzed intermittently from inside my purse, which signaled incoming messages. I followed my mother up the marble steps as I fished my phone out.

Axel had written on Instagram: *Are you getting my texts anymore? I just tried calling you and it goes straight to voicemail. Did you fucking block my number?*

AXEL: How the fuck do you go from engaged to taking a break to blocking my number?

AXEL: Cora, answer me!

Nausea churned through me, making the hairs on my arm stand on end. I hadn't blocked him. I didn't need to guess who had.

"Cora, are you okay?" my mother asked, but her voice sounded a million miles away. I brushed past her, heading for the half bath just inside the main foyer.

I burst through the door and bolted for the pristine toilet, yanking open the lid so I could ingloriously expel another round of bile.

I collapsed in front of the toilet and gagged a couple more times.

My mother's heels clicked across the smooth gray tiles. The bathroom door swung shut a moment later, my mother on the wrong side of it.

"Are you pregnant?"

I pinched my eyes shut. "No." *I'm just life-shatteringly distraught.*

"If you are, you have options," she went on in a low, calculated voice. "And if it's his, I suggest we take care of this immediately."

"I...I'm not..."

"Don't be ashamed," my mother counseled. "We've all been there. But you should know that there will be limits to our support if it *is* his and you choose to have it."

There it was again. The illusion of choice. I pushed back from the toilet, drawing a deep breath.

"I'm not pregnant. I'm just fucking sad."

Her lips pursed together. I rose unsteadily and she gave me a quick squeeze on the shoulder.

"You will get past this," she said, searing me with a meaningful look. And right there, I could tell she was trying. "It hurts for a while. But it goes away eventually." Her throat bobbed, and then she repeated, "We've all been there."

I wasn't sure whether to thank her or push her away. So I shuffled to the sink to splash water on my face.

"I guess the house is mine now," I croaked. "Once you puke in it, it's yours."

My mother tutted. "Don't be crass, dear. I'll meet you outside."

I ground my teeth as I stared at my reflection. I'd spent hours refining my appearance today, to look healthy, alive, put-together. But beneath the veneer of foundation and setting spray and long-lasting mascara, I was a little girl who just wanted to be held.

Axel would have laughed at my joke and held me until the next morning.

Here in my perfect new stucco paradise, the cold winds of loneliness threatened to freeze me on the spot.

My phone buzzed from the marble countertop. I knew it was Axel, because I'd be connected to him until the day I died.

AXEL: I'm leaving for LA tonight. We're going to solve this, Cora.

AXEL: You've got to let me fix this.

But there was no solution. Not for him.

Everything had already been arranged, and he couldn't be part of the picture.

CHAPTER THIRTEEN

CORA

The next twenty-four hours crept by painfully, each hour an eternity as I awaited whatever came next. Early on Saturday morning, after never fully achieving sleep the night before, I decided I needed to strike a compromise with my father. I pulled myself out of bed at seven a.m., brewed the darkest coffee I could muster, and called.

"Why the early call?" my father asked in lieu of a greeting. "Don't tell me you got locked out of your new house already."

The churn of my stomach forced me to dive headfirst. "Axel is on his way to LA."

"And?"

"He's coming to see me."

"Why the *hell* would you invite him to see you after our agreement?" His voice shook with barely concealed rage.

My insides plummeted as I studied the gray stone flooring of my kitchen. Everything was gorgeous in this place. It just wasn't what I would have chosen. "I didn't invite him. I'm telling you because I'm trying to be a decent human being. But the truth is, I need to see him one last time. Just to end it."

"You told me it was ended."

"It's a process," I snapped. "We've been together for three years."

"Three years is nothing."

"It's a lot to us," I said, my voice catching. "It's not like a light you turn off with a switch. There are feelings involved. These things are...delicate." I couldn't believe I needed to explain this to a grown man.

"Whatever it may be, you're officially in a business situation. Business trumps emotions. How many times have you heard this in your life? When are you finally going to get it?"

Hot tears crowded the edges of my vision. "This is an exception to the rule. Axel isn't business. Whatever you feel about it, we've had a relationship for years—"

"And relationships end. You move on. You're moving on. End of story. Is this all you called about?"

I was being dismissed. Everything in his tone said *time to go*.

"I'm telling you I just need one last encounter with him," I said in a low, shaky voice. After the past few weeks, my nerves were frayed, all my reserves of composure emptied. "A half hour. That's it. The only reason he's coming out here is because I haven't been able to transition smoothly."

"That sounds like a lack of decisive management."

His intentional insensitivity crossed over from ridiculous to infuriating. "Jesus, Dad! He was my boyfriend, not a damn employee! I can't just manage my way out of this."

"But that's where you're wrong, Cora. You can manage your way out of anything. This is one of the lessons you'll need to learn quickly before you take over. Everything is a matter of strategy. And if you're wise—which I've fought like hell to make sure you will be—your strategy for your romantic partner will be closely intertwined with your business plan. When a marriage is arranged correctly, the ideal mate isn't that far from salaried employee anyway."

Sadness swept through me in thick swells that threatened to choke. *When a marriage is arranged correctly.*

"So you think Mom is a salaried employee?" I whispered.

"She's my perfect companion," he replied, undeterred. "In family and business. What more could I ask for?"

"Do you love her?"

"We are very happy together."

I pinched my eyes shut. "Please just let me see Axel one more time."

"Absolutely not. Hope you're settling into the new house."

The line went dead.

A sob escaped me, and I clamped a hand over my mouth. I was so tired of crying. Tired of grieving. Tired of this bone-heavy sadness.

Yet I felt doomed to live in this state forever. Ever since Chris had taken his own life, things had gotten worse and worse.

And now I was forced to snuff out the only bright spot in my existence.

I swiped through my phone dully. There had to be a game plan lurking somewhere in the cracks. I knew Axel had to be close. If he'd left NYC last night, he was probably due to arrive within the hour. And maybe that's why I hadn't slept last night, knowing that Axel grew closer with each passing second. Shrinking the distance between our hearts. Putting us within arm's reach yet still an entire world away.

I looked at my phone without knowing what I even looked for. Axel would go to the old condo. He didn't know that I'd moved. That had been by design.

I had no way to get to the condo myself. Randall wouldn't take me—I didn't need to ask to know that my father had already put that address on the forbidden list. And after what happened with my housekeeper, I could better imagine the ways my father kept tabs on me from every angle.

The vice I lived in grew tighter. Every passing day.

And it felt tighter than ever inside this beautiful home, infused with someone else's taste and life.

In here, Cora Margulis didn't matter. She was just a pawn in a bigger, more important game.

And the worst part was that I had chosen this. I wasn't insane; I wasn't unwell; there was no psychiatrist who could attest to my unfit mental state. I'd fucking chosen this, with my own brain and free will.

What have you gotten into?

I drew deep breaths as I stared at my coffee, searching for answers in the caramel color.

Axel is going to the condo.

How could I be there with him?

The idea formed less as a lightning strike and more as a glacial revelation. The doorbell app was still on my phone. Which meant that I could *see* him, at the very least.

My heart rate picked up as I swiped through screens. I pressed the icon, holding my breath.

The front porch of my old condo, peaceful and empty, filled the screen. I turned on the sound and could even hear the distant twitter of birds.

Holy shit.

I set my phone on its charging dock, and glued my eyes to the scene at my old place. I'd stand here all day and watch if I had to—anything for a glimpse of Axel. This was the worst goodbye I could have imagined for us. Not even in my worst nightmares had I foreseen this terrible conclusion.

I just hoped there was some way I could make things right for him someday. Make things right for *me*.

I drifted around my kitchen for the next hour, making juice and popping almonds, constantly listening for any sign of movement at the condo. A couple fake-outs put me on edge—a distant shout down the street, the shuffling feet of the mailman.

Seconds turned into hours, and I wanted to crawl out of my skin more with each tick of the clock. Axel had to be close. Where was he?

Another pot of coffee had just finished brewing when I heard the footsteps. The heavy breathing. The *thud thud thud* against the front door of my old condo.

"Cora. It's me." The rasp of Axel's voice sent my coffee mug clattering to the floor. It broke into pieces at my feet, but I couldn't look away from the screen on my phone.

"Cora!" He knocked again, harder. "Cora, I'm here."

Silent seconds trudged by, and he propped the palms of his hands against my front door. "Cora. *Please*." He pounded the door three more times.

Axel shook his head, raking his fingers through the messy length of his hair. He propped his hands on his hips, looking back toward the street, which allowed me a glimpse of his face.

Oh, how stressed he looked. How drawn and sagging and empty. I swallowed back a wave of nausea—too familiar to me at this point—as I absorbed the physical effects of what I'd done to this man. To *my* man. The man I supposedly loved more than anything or anyone in the world.

There was no one living I loved more.

But in a twisted way, me hurting him would benefit him. He would dodge the wrath of Allan Margulis. Axel thought my father's opinion didn't matter, but he was wrong. There was no escaping my father when he was determined to make good on his word.

His promise to ruin Axel scared the living fuck out of me.

"Come on, Cora. Open up!" The gruff shout of his voice snapped me out of my stupor. He headed into the landscaping then, cupping his hands around his face as he peered into the window of the front room. "What the fuck? Where is all the furniture?"

When he returned to the cement pad of the porch, he interlaced his fingers behind his head, staring at the door. I couldn't see his face, and I would have given almost anything to do so.

"Cora, are you in there? I just need you to open up," he finally said, his arms dropping to his sides. He looked around, finally locating the camera of my doorbell monitor.

And this time, he looked straight at me. "Please talk to me. Just talk to me, babe. We can figure this out. I promise you." He sounded broken, a breath away from tears. Every ounce of emotion swam across his face, a blatant parade for me to see.

You did this to him. And now you can't undo it.

"I don't know what I did wrong, Cora, but I promise you I will fix it. Do you hear me? We are bigger than this. We are better than this. You can't do this to me. You can't just slam the door in my face and run away."

Tears streamed down my cheeks as he spoke. I reached for him, grasping air, my heart splintering into fragments as I watched his beautiful face contort in pain. I finally came to and fumbled with my phone, pulling up the button for the intercom.

"Axel," I choked out.

"Cora." His voice cracked and he pinched the bridge of his nose. "Thank the fucking lord. Can we talk? Where's all the furniture? What's going on?"

"I-I don't live there anymore," I said, a sob hiccupping out of me. "My dad got me a new house. I haven't been able to contact you or your brothers through my phone. He locked everything down." The words were pouring out of me, desperate to say everything in what felt like the few remaining seconds until my father clamped down again.

"Jesus Christ, Cora," Axel moaned, dragging his hands down his face. "You're his fucking hostage."

"Axel, you should go," I said shakily. Security would be arriving any minute. I couldn't believe we were actually communicating, and through technology that my father paid for.

"I know your dad is giving you shit about us," he started, his voice cracking as he looked directly into the camera again. "And I've been thinking about what you said...second thoughts and all. And that's fine, that's fine, I just—" He paused, tugging at the front of his hair as he looked to the street and back at the camera. "Can't we talk about it?"

My tears had morphed into sobs. He deserved that and so much more. Desperation rose like a tornado inside me, whipping away my breath and my focus.

"I don't want to beg you like this forever, Cora," Axel said, his voice cracking again. "Are you there?"

"I'm here," I said. My father's words rang in my head, where they lived permanently, staining my existence. *Utterly inferior in every conceivable way.* That's what he thought about Axel, but I knew the reality of it. Axel was the only man who had ever fought for me. Who would pay for a cross country flight to get to me even though he had barely enough money to live on. I couldn't keep stealing his love and energy when it would go nowhere.

It only made me feel worse. More selfish. More useless.

"Meet up with me." The plea straining his voice prompted another round of tears. "Just let me see your beautiful face one more time, babe. I know we can work this out."

"We can't, Axel," I whispered, my voice thick with emotion. "There's just no way."

"Don't say that—"

"You don't get it," I snapped. "I was wrong. I thought it could work, but it can't. Okay? I was wrong about us. I love you, Axel," I choked out, feeling lightheaded and like I weighed a thousand pounds at the same time. I was shocked I could speak through all the tears. "But love isn't enough."

He used the collar of his T-shirt to wipe at his upper lip. Then he swiped a tear away from his cheek. "Jesus fucking Christ. Do you hear yourself?"

He paced the porch a couple of times and then pushed his palms against the front door again. Then he unleashed his fury, pounding so hard it seemed the door might crack in two. *Bam bam bam!* Each slam punctured my heart over here in my new house just outside Stanford, and I covered my face with my hands and sobbed.

"Cora, do you hear yourself? You're crying. He's got to be making you say this shit. What is he holding over you?"

"Nothing," I forced out on the heels of a new, body-wracking sob. "I don't know what else to tell you." A text message flashed across the top of my screen.

ALLAN: Stop engaging with him!!!

I could imagine him trying like hell to shut down the app from wherever he was. He'd been probably watching this entire time, calling IT support, melting down in his quietly lethal way. I had seconds left with Axel. If that.

"Please just try to forget about me," I whispered, cupping my face with my hands. My cheeks hurt from how contorted my face was with the sobs. Ugly crying at its finest. "Move on."

Axel's breathing grew heavier, and then there were additional footsteps. Two men stepped up on the porch.

My father's security guards had arrived.

"You need to leave . Immediately," one declared brusquely.

"Big fucking surprise," Axel said, not bothering to hide the emotion clogging his throat. I'd never seen him like this before. So broken. So raw. So absolutely devastated.

"Please step off the property," the other guard said.

"Just give me a second," Axel said, his shoulders sagging. "I'm in the middle of something."

"You're not on the list of approved visitors, and you're going to have to leave. Now." The third warning was the final one. Both guards grabbed for Axel. He dodged, but against four burly arms, he had no prayer of evading them. They captured him easily, though he struggled against their grip.

"Jesus fucking Christ," Axel spat, lurching to free himself. "Allan's hired grunts, huh? Cora, do you see this? Why won't you fucking fight for me? After all we've been through?"

Axel continued railing against me and my father as the guards dragged him, but the farther they took him, the less I could hear. They carried him away, arms hooked under his armpits, until finally the camera showed a tranquil scene on the front porch once more.

Birds twittered. The arborvitae, pruned and flawless. Lace lichen climbing around the corner of the condo. Everything picture perfect.

The truth lay beyond the edges of the frame.

Shards of our hearts were scattered everywhere, just out of sight. The broken remains of our promises. Our hopes. Our expectations.

None of them could hold up to what life had dealt me. The impossible pressure my life path had in store.

I could only imagine how wrecked Axel would be. He wouldn't recover quickly from this. Neither would I.

I was already beating myself up over it. Maybe I should have tamped down my feelings in the beginning. Maybe we could have avoided all this pain and heartbreak and life-path incompatibility if I'd just seen the writing on the wall when we met. And now it was my fault Axel was unraveling, looked sunken and hollow. The reason he'd been stressing and worried and distracted.

Just like it was my fault for not trying harder to save Chris. It was my fault I'd gotten wrapped up in my own world. I'd opted to hang with my friends the night he'd sent me his last text. I hadn't protected him from the unyielding glare of this world we'd been born into. Even though I was younger, I'd always handled it better. And I'd always known that.

I bore every ounce of this burden.

A burden I could only bear for the sake of the two men I loved more than life itself.

CHAPTER FOURTEEN

AXEL

THREE MONTHS LATER

"I really wish you'd reconsider," Trace said, his dark brows drawn together.

Damian watched me, frowning, from off to the side of our worn living room couch. They stood above me like this was an intervention, and I guess it was in a way.

They wanted me to continue pursuing my MBA while I still had a chance to wrap it up, once and for all.

I, however, completely fucking disagreed.

"Listen, I know you guys want me to be all noble and right-eous in my quest to kiss the almighty wealthy asshole, but I'm not going to." I crossed my arms, leaning back into the couch. After Cora broke things off before Christmas, I'd all but for-mally dropped out of my courses. I sure as fuck hadn't paid the tuition for the last semester, either. But because they were good brothers, they cared about the increasing amount of time I spent pacing my bedroom and drawing up business strategies.

"We didn't have enough money for all three of us to complete our degrees," I went on. "Honestly, I got what I need out of the program. I can't concentrate on the bullshit theories anymore. I just need to jump headfirst into our business. I'm ready."

Concentration on anything that wasn't actionable progress was a threat. A possibility that I'd slip down the greased slope of self-pity, down into the well of longing that still burbled inside me. Any misstep was a chance to completely lose my shit again about Cora.

I'd spent the past few months in unbearable agony, hashing and rehashing every word we'd shared in the last month of our relationship. Remembering the sheer joy on her face the night I'd asked her to marry me, and then picking apart every second after that, trying to work out what had changed her mind.

Her father wielded immense power, but he didn't control her emotions.

Cora may have been coerced, but she'd made the decision on her own.

"Think about it this way," Trace said, raking his hand through his thick, dark hair. "We're a team. A trio. And we all need to have our goddamn MBAs."

"I'm done playing their game," I said, kicking my feet onto the coffee table. "Two out of three with MBAs ain't bad, gentleman. Now they can take it or leave it, and I'll convince them to take it. I need to be our salesman, and I could do this job without even my bachelor's."

Damian peered at me over the top of his round glasses. "You're going to be our point man for every single business transaction...and you want to walk in there without your fucking MBA?"

"Yes," I huffed. "I'll go finish it someday if you want. But for now? We need to get this business off the ground. We don't have the cash for both Damian and me to walk in May now that you're out, Trace. I will be the virgin sacrifice here."

Trace snorted. "Yeah. Virgin my ass."

I cleared my throat. It had taken about a month for my hope to finally die out, then I'd turned to the only outlet I knew: endless pussy. For three weeks I went hog wild, fucking my way through most of Lower Manhattan once it really hit me that Cora was gone forever.

Three months in, the hurt still hadn't lessened. It had only spread to new extremes. Like poison ivy, stretching silent and territorial, warning any human that dared cross its path. And it was twisting itself into new shapes. Pushing me into scary situations. Prompting new types of thoughts. Breaking barriers that I'd previously considered impassable.

And for how angry I still was, how hurt and heartbroken? I couldn't say that I'd turn her down if she showed up at my door tomorrow. As Cora had once said: *it doesn't get easier, you just get used to it.*

I wasn't sure I'd ever get used to this.

It was so fucking wrong. The whole situation reeked of shit. I'd never been so confused before, not even after entering the foster system and grappling for roots alongside Damian, mourning the loss of our younger sisters.

What happened with Cora was a new depth of loss, something I'd never felt before and never wanted to fucking feel again.

"I don't know what you guys want me to say," I went on, dragging my hands down my face. "I've wanted to quit for two semesters. And now, financially, one of us has to drop out. We won't get our dividends until the quarter after graduation, so I'm willing to do it. And in the meantime, I've been working from sunup to sundown to get our shit moving in the right direction. I promise you that.

MBA or not, these motherfuckers won't know what hit them. And honestly? I want to show them what a Kentucky boy can do *without* an MBA."

A smile tugged at Trace's lips. "You know, the scary part is that even when you have outlandish, completely ridiculous ideas, I still believe you."

"Then I'm doing my job."

Damian took off his glasses and spent a moment cleaning them with the hem of his shirt. When he put them back on, he leaned so close I could see the yellow flecks in his green eyes.

"You really want to do it this way?"

"Yes."

Damian's jaw flexed. "Fine. But you do not have my permission to fuck this up. There is too much riding on this. We're not just trying to pay for school and get out of debt. This is for Jordan and Kaylee."

Conjuring our younger sisters' names was a sobering move. I averted my eyes, studying the constellation of city lights visible outside our fifth floor window. Silence throbbed between us, the energy wavering between tense and somber.

"You don't think I know that?" I finally forced out.

"Of course I think you know that," Damian said, softer this time. "But I'm saying we need to give this business our all. It *has* to work. And as far as I can see, we've got one shot."

"Whatever we do to establish ourselves," Trace said, "is going to become a part of our reputation. We need to tread carefully. But we need to act decisively."

"I've got decisiveness. And I've got my rubber boots, so I can tread carefully though whatever shit people decide they want to sling our way. Hell, between those two things and three-quarters of a degree from Columbia Business School, I think I'm as ready as I'll ever be to head the firm as CEO. A piece of paper from the university isn't gonna change much. The three of us can change the world."

Damian nodded, finally backing down. He walked slowly around the living room, arms crossed tightly.

"We *will* change the world," he promised.

"As long as we're clear headed. Focused. And we can stay out of the spotlight," Trace added.

"All publicity is good publicity," I said. "We're bound to make it to the tabloids once we're rich enough. It's just a matter of time."

"Fine. Limited spotlight then," Trace conceded. "At least minimize the spotlight for non-business endeavors."

"That's a good distinction," Damian pointed out. "Because the algorithm I cooked up is going to turn some heads. We're not going to be able to fly under the radar, so our noses need to be clean." When Damian talked that way about what he cooked up while coding, I believed him. The man was a genius. He could hack into any computer and had even gotten into Pentagon files once for fun in undergrad. The algorithm he'd created would become the basis of our wealth management approach.

In other words, it was what would make us become *le crème de la crème* of finance.

"I'm fine with that." I squeezed my knees, every inch of me crawling with desire to get this show on the road. Every step closer to success equaled more distance between me and the memory of Cora. My goal was to eradicate her completely from my waking thoughts. At this rate, it might take a decade to get there. "I'll keep my one-night stands to a dull roar. And we don't even have to worry about you two in that department." I smirked.

"Oh, no?" Trace lifted a brow. "You act like our dicks have fallen off."

"Because they have." I reached out to punch Trace in the crotch, but he caught my fist. We had a brief battle of strength before I ceded.

"We get what we need," Damian said.

"Which is what, a pocket pussy?" I teased.

Damian's lips thinned. "Just because I don't flaunt my cock like you do these days doesn't mean I don't have any fun."

"Dude, if I don't flaunt my cock, I'll go crazy," I told him earnestly. Sadness gripped me again, a painful chokehold. "I need my coping mechanism."

"Let him have it," Trace chided Damian. "At least it isn't drugs or alcohol."

on occasion," I clarified. Truth was, I'd been downing way more beer and whiskey than ever before. But some nights, it was the only way I could make thoughts of Cora stop. Sex turned my brain off for nights when the memories were the loudest. Alcohol numbed the pain when I felt like I'd drown in how much I still loved her.

And deep down inside, I wasn't sure this feeling would ever truly go away. I knew time healed all wounds, but this was a nasty gash that had cut into a place that might not ever recover.

"Point is, I'm ready to go all in on this. *Now.* Because the alternative isn't pretty. I'm sick of being cash strapped and waiting for dividends to hit the bank account. I'm done paying for Chinese food with crypto because our assets are tied up until whatever random future date. I want us to have a fucking penthouse with a view and so much cash that we're donating to charities *weekly*. Nobody will be afraid to invest with us, because Fairchild Enterprises will become *the* name for wealth. That's a fucking promise."

"God, I love it when you get on these tangents," Trace said with a grin.

"And with this algorithm, we're going to do right by Jordan and Kaylee. I wasn't kidding when I said these rich assholes won't know what hit 'em. We'll be pumping their own money back into the communities that need the most support."

"Wouldn't it be fun to personally investigate each client, figure out their pain point, and put the money there?" Damian said, an evil sparkle lighting up his eyes.

"Oh, I like when you get devilish," I said.

"Food for thought," Damian said with a shrug. "If we've got the manpower, we could figure out where we feed their extra-vestments." *Extra-vestments* was our inside term. It meant the skimmed percentages we planned to take, not as our service fee, but as our charity fee, built into the investment schema so that our clients had no idea they were silently feeding money into social services and charities.

It was a moral gray area and one we were pleased to enter. After all, Trace would invest the money so well that our clients would have no room to complain. They'd be missing nothing. And we'd be taking what looked like a service charge.

Win-win.

"You know I'm down for that," I said. "And I'd be ecstatic if we could get Allan Margulis as a client down the road and send an even larger portion of his profits straight to the Kentucky foster care system."

Damian snickered. "Yeah. Good luck snagging him."

"I'm serious," I said.

"I know you are," Trace replied, sending me a stern look. "But we're not scouting Dickhead Dad, okay? He's not our target."

I cleared my throat to prevent myself from answering how I really wanted.

Allan Margulis *was* my target. How could he not be?

He'd pissed on me from day one. Overlooked me in every way possible. Talked down to me to my face. Kept his daughter from seeing me. And no doubt a whole list of even worse things that I didn't know about. *Yet.*

Because I would know about them.

No, Allan Margulis wasn't just a target, he and his whole slimy empire were *the* target.

I wasn't content letting him steamroll me into oblivion. Allan Margulis had nasty practices, and I wouldn't allow them to dictate my future. In fact, it was precisely because he wanted to declare himself master of my destiny that my motivation had sharpened into a dagger.

I'd promised him I'd get my business up and running to prove myself and provide for his daughter.

Now that promise had become a threat. He needed to hope like hell I wouldn't make good on my word. Because once my business catapulted into the stratosphere, I'd be coming for him.

For all of them.

I didn't know how, but I'd make sure I got what I wanted out of the Margulis family.

Revenge.

THE END

Axel and Cora's story is FAR from over! Find out what happens eight years down the road in *The Price of Revenge*, the first full-length novel of the series.

ACKNOWLEDGEMENTS

This book would not have been possible without the gracious flexibility of my husband Jorge and our beautiful boys, who now find it a familiar sight when I bust out my computer on road trips and/or during dinner.

Special thanks to my amazing beta squad, who always find time to give me their thoughts, feedback, and ideas for improving my work. Special shout-out to Rebecca Hamilton, whose incredible methods helped shape this entire series.

There are so many people and influences behind the scenes, for which I am constantly grateful. And most importantly, thank you to everyone who has supported me throughout the years by sharing, purchasing, or reading my work. It means more to me than I could possibly express.

LET'S STAY CONNECTED!

Sign up to <u>my newsletter</u>, where you'll receive information about upcoming releases, sales, and other exciting news.

Or join my reader group, EMBER'S BLOSSOMS, to hang out up-close and personal! Early looks at new covers, exclusive access to ARC sign-ups, and more.

FACEBOOK

INSTAGRAM

GOODREADS

BOOKBUB

http://www.emberleighromance.com/

And before you go...
Please consider leaving an honest review about this book! Even just a few words or a line mean so much to us authors.

ALSO BY EMBER LEIGH

THE BAD BOYS OF WALL STREET
The Price of Revenge
The Price of Passion
The Price of Infamy
The Price of Forever

WINTER HARBOR
(co-written with Whitley Cox)
The Bastard Heir
The Asshole Heir
The Rebel Heir
The Matchmaking Heirs

THE BAYSHORE SERIES
Make Me Lose
Make Me Fall
Make Me Yours
Make Me Choose
Make Me Hot
Make Me Smile

THE BREAKING SERIES
Breaking the Rules

Changing the Game
Breaking the Sinner
Breaking the Habit
Breaking the Fall